BENNY

Also by Barbara Cohen

Bitter Herbs and Honey
The Carp in the Bathtub
Thank You, Jackie Robinson
Where's Florrie?

BENNY

by Barbara Cohen

Lothrop, Lee & Shepard Co.
A Division of William Morrow & Co., Inc.

New York

1   2   3   4   5   6   7   8   9   10
Library of Congress Cataloging in Publication Data
Cohen, Barbara.
    Benny.
    SUMMARY: A German refugee's unhappiness affords Benny Rifkind a
chance to show his family that he has concerns other than baseball and the
1939 World's Fair.
    [1. Jews—Fiction.   2. United States—Social life and customs—1918-1945
—Fiction]   I. Title.
PZ7.C6595Be   [Fic]   77-242
    ISBN 0-688-41804-X   ISBN 0-688-51804-4 lib. bdg.

**Again
for
Gene**

one

"Illegitimus non carborundum," my brother Sheldon used to say in that phony Latin he and his friends liked to put on. They used to say other dumb things too, like "Piggo, piggere, squealy, squawkum," and "failo, failere, failo, flunkum." In those days everyone who thought he might go to college took at least two years of Latin in high school. I know it's not that way anymore.

"Illegitimus non carborundum—don't let the bastards grind you down." So far as I was concerned, my brother Sheldon was the worst bastard of all, and he ground me down all the time. He wasn't the only one; nearly everyone else did too, except maybe my sister Evelyn, my Aunt Goldie, and my buddy Henry Silverberg. Three people on my team and everyone else on the other side—my mother, my father, my teacher Mrs. Elfand, all the other guys in the sixth grade at Albert Payson Terhune Elementary School, and Sheldon. Especially Sheldon.

This one morning I was just beginning to float up out of sleep when I heard a voice screaming, "Sit still, damn you. Sit still so I can get you. How can I get you if you won't sit still?" It shocked me awake. It was my mother's voice. In the whole twelve years of my life, I'd never heard my mother say *damn.* Nor my father either, to tell the truth.

I heard a lot of clumping around too, in my parents' bedroom. I looked at the clock on the night table next to Sheldon's side of the bed. It was eight-thirty, so my father was already downstairs in the store. It had to be my mother making all that noise, and that was definitely no good. My mother had just had a hysterectomy. That's when they take out a lady's womb—the part where her babies grow. In Ma's case the babies had been Sheldon, Evvie, and me. Sheldon had explained it all to me. Ma wasn't supposed to get excited or move around too much.

I shook Sheldon, who was still asleep next to me. "Wake up," I urged. "Wake up right now."

Sheldon opened one bleary eye and groaned. "What the hell do you want, Benny? Dammit, why can't you leave me alone?" Sheldon swore all the time, but he yelled at me if he ever heard me doing it. Sheldon thought he was my boss, like an extra father. I think one father is enough for any human being.

"Don't you hear all that racket?" I insisted. "Something's the matter with Ma."

Then Sheldon sat up and listened too. "Yeah," he said, jumping out of bed. "We'd better find out what's happening."

"In their room?" I asked, shocked all over again. "Go in there?" No one went into my parents' bedroom without a specific invitation. It had to be that way if they were ever to get any privacy in our little apartment.

"Sometimes I wonder how anyone as stupid as you can live," Sheldon said. "Come on." He opened the door of our room. I followed. He knocked on the door opposite, hesitantly at first, but then louder when there was no answer.

"What's the matter?" my mother called. She sounded normal enough.

"Nothing," Sheldon answered. "What's the matter with you?"

"With me? What could be the matter with me? No more than usual." She opened the door, still wearing her shapeless flannel nightgown. Once it had had blue flowers on it, but it had been washed so often that now they were just sort of grayish spots against the slightly less gray background. In one hand she carried a fly swatter, like a spear.

"Darn fly," she said, waving the swatter at us. "He's kept me up since your father left. How'm I going to get better if I can't get any sleep?"

I was relieved. "Boy," I said, "you had us worried. We couldn't imagine who you were swearing at."

"I never swear," she said. "Don't you."

"Oh, I never do either," Sheldon said. "Did you get the fly?"

"No." She handed him the swatter and we followed her into the bedroom. A huge black horsefly was resting on the window shade. "Wait till he moves," she said. "I don't want you knocking down the shade." But Sheldon walked softly to the window and with one light, sharp smack killed him dead.

"Get a piece of wet toilet paper from the bathroom," he said to me, "and clean it up."

"Why me?" I protested. "You had the fun of killing it. Why do I have to do the dirty work?"

"Go ahead, Benny," my mother said. "Why aren't you in the store? It's almost nine o'clock."

"Benny get out of bed before someone makes him?" Sheldon asked derisively. "You must be kidding."

"This morning I woke *you* up," I reminded him.

"I wish you were a girl," Sheldon complained.

"Then I'd get to sleep in the sun parlor and Evelyn would have to share a room with you. Ma, couldn't we at least have twin beds?"

"You know I can't fit twin beds in that room," she replied. "I've told you that."

"Bunk beds, then," I suggested.

"And worry all night about one of you falling out? I don't sleep as it is."

"But Ma," I said, "we're big."

"Clean up the window shade, Benny, and get down to the store. What do you think we are, millionaires, we can run around buying beds?"

Of course Sheldon had to stick in his two cents. "Nine o'clock," he said, "and you're still not helping Pop."

"You haven't helped Pop in six months," I pointed out.

"You know Sheldon has to study," Ma said. "Now get downstairs. But clean the shade first."

We went back to our room to dress. "You shouldn't aggravate Ma like that," Sheldon scolded as he shut the door behind him. "Not in her condition."

"Oh, shut up," I said. "Leave me alone."

"Don't swear, Benny. Ma told you not to swear."

"*Shut up* is not swearing." I decided to go clean the shade before getting dressed. I took my clothes with me. I'd get dressed in the bathroom, away from the endless sound of Sheldon's voice.

After I had gotten rid of the fly's splatted carcass and put on my clothes, I went into the kitchen for breakfast. Ma had gone back to bed. Sheldon was already at his desk in the living room. Only Evelyn was with me. She put a piece of buttered challah left over from last night and a glass of milk down in front of me. "If you want," she said, "I'll make you an egg."

"No thanks," I said. "I'm in a hurry. I got to get down to the store."

"Chew your food," she insisted. "Another two minutes won't make any difference." She sat down opposite me and began to drink coffee from a Bosco Bear mug. She had just started drinking coffee recently, when she'd begun running our household. Ma didn't like her drinking it too much, but she didn't try to stop her.

"What do you think I ought to make for supper tonight?" Evvie asked me conversationally. It wouldn't matter what I answered. She'd make whatever she wanted anyway.

"Hey, listen, Evvie," I said, "don't you ever get tired of doing all the cooking and cleaning around here? I bet all your friends are going to the movies this afternoon."

"Me too," Evelyn said. "We're going to see John Wayne and Claire Trevor in *Stagecoach*. I'll clean this morning. And supper will only take me an hour or so after I get home. I've had so much practice I've gotten awfully fast."

"Do you think Ma will ever get better?" I asked. "Enough better to take care of the house and help Pop in the store and do all the things she used to do?"

"Of course she will," Evelyn replied firmly. "It just takes time, that's all. She was only operated on six weeks ago. But you know, Benny, things will never go back to being the way they were. We're growing up, and we have to help. They're getting older and they need our help."

"When you and Sheldon were twelve," I said, "you didn't have to help."

"We helped plenty," Evelyn said. "Come on, Benny, you've gotten away with murder all your life. The youngest always does."

"That's what Sheldon says, all the time."

"Well," Evelyn admitted, "he does exaggerate. But he doesn't actually *lie*."

"You may think it's easy, being the youngest," I said, "but it isn't. Especially if you're sort of dumb, like me."

"You're smart enough," Evvie replied. I didn't think she sounded too sure. "Who says you're not?"

"Sheldon says it all the time. Ma too. She says I never do anything right. And you gotta admit, my marks aren't very good. Not like Sheldon's."

"No one gets marks like Sheldon," Evelyn said, making a face.

"My marks aren't as good as yours either."

"You just haven't caught up with yourself yet," she explained. "You've grown six inches in two years. Your brain can't cope with that. Give it time."

I looked down at my wrists and hands. They were hanging endlessly past the cuffs of my plaid flannel shirt. "Yeah." I grinned. "Sometimes it seems as if my arms and my legs don't even belong to me."

"Like Alice in Wonderland," Evvie said.

"Like who? Oh yeah, that girl in the book. Well, you see, that's what I mean."

"No, I don't see," Evelyn said. "The world is full of geniuses who never read *Alice in Wonderland*."

"Yeah?" I didn't really believe her, but I was in too much of a hurry to discuss it. I gulped down the rest of the milk and got up. "See ya," I said.

Evelyn nodded. "Don't worry so much, Benny," she said. "Everything'll be all right."

"I hope so." I threw my rolled-up paper napkin at the garbage pail. Naturally, I missed.

"Don't worry," she said again. "I'll get it. You go." She smiled. "Go ahead." So I ran out, leaving her there, slowly sipping her coffee.

two

When I opened the door into the store, I saw my father sitting on a stepladder behind the counter reading the paper, with a worried look on his face. If Evelyn worried because I worried, she was going to turn gray worrying about Pop worrying. My father worried even more than my mother, though he didn't talk about it nearly as much. He worried about more things. My whole family worried all the time, even Sheldon.

"What's the matter, Pop?" I asked. "You look worried."

"I don't know where this business is going to

15

end," my father replied. He pointed to the big head-
line on the front page of the paper. *HITLER DE-
MANDS DANZIG.* He shook his head. "No one
seems willing to stop that man. And it's going to
end up for the Jews such a pogrom it'll make the
ones my father saw in Russia look like Fourth of
July picnics."

"Don't you think maybe the paper exaggerates?"
I tried to comfort him. I had heard him complain
lots of times that reporters made things out to be
worse than they were just to sell newspapers.

"Don't be stupid, Benny," Pop said. "The newspapers don't even tell the whole story. They're
afraid to. Too many powerful pro-German influ-
ences in this country. But we know better. We've
talked to refugees. How about the one from Mann-
heim who visited Moe and Goldie in February?
The people who brought that little boy who's some
kind of distant cousin to Moe? Remember the hor-
ror stories they told?"

I didn't remember. I hadn't listened to the grown-
ups talking that Sunday afternoon Pop had dragged
us over to Aunt Goldie's to meet the Germans. Ma
had told me to "be nice to the little German boy,"
so how was I supposed to know what the grown-
ups had been talking about? "The little German
boy" was as old as I was and the snottiest kid I'd
ever met. For a whole afternoon I had to listen to
him complain in a voice like Paul Lukas' about how
rotten everything was in the United States. The

schools were too easy, he said, the people too rude, the games too stupid. That day was the first time I couldn't wait to get out of my Aunt Goldie's house.

But Pop remembered everything the Germans had said that afternoon. "Forced out of their homes. Forced to give up their businesses or their jobs," he agonized. "Forced to leave school. Some of them sent off to camps where no one ever hears from them again! And still most of them won't leave. 'We're Germans,' they say. 'We're Germans first.' Even that couple at Moe's house—they left, but they wouldn't hear a word against Germany. 'The Germans will get over Hitler,' they said. 'They'll throw him out. Then we can go back where we belong.'"

"I hope they do go," I said. "That snotty kid didn't have anything good to say about this country."

But suddenly Pop was on the refugees' side. "It's hard to come to a new country," he said. "It's hard to start a new life. You should try to understand, Benny."

"O.K., Pop," I agreed. "If that's the way you want it."

My father folded the paper neatly and put it on the shelf behind the counter. "Bring in the eggs," he said. "I've been so busy reading the paper, I haven't even gotten started."

The egg man came from the country twice a

week and left enough eggs to last until his next delivery in the back room behind the store. My father brought them up front a crate at a time. He said it was cooler in the back room and they kept better there.

I went into the back room, picked up an egg crate, and turned to carry it into the store. Suddenly I heard the back door slam and a voice call, "Hey, Benny!"

I was so startled, I dropped the egg crate. I turned again and saw Henry Silverberg standing at the door. "Cripes, Henry!" I shouted. "Now see what you made me do!" The egg crate was at my feet. From its corners the sticky yellow goop of broken eggs was oozing.

"I made you do it?" Henry said. "How did I make you do it?" But he came all the way into the room and knelt down to try to help me clean up. Really, Henry was a good kid.

"Maybe I can save some of them," I said as I opened the top of the crate. "Maybe they didn't *all* break." But inside the carton only a few eggs remained intact. The others, if not broken, had big cracks in them. My father would have to sell them at less than he had paid for them.

"What happened, Benny?" I looked up and saw Pop standing in the doorway. He must have heard the carton thud to the floor.

"I dropped the crate, Pop. Henry slammed the back door and it startled me."

"Are they all broken?"

"A lot of them are just cracked."

He looked in the case. "The bottom layers will be worse," he said."For that crate of eggs that cost me six dollars and sixty cents, I'll be lucky if I get four and a half."

"I'm sorry, Pop. I'm really sorry."

"Sorry doesn't help, Benny. Sorry doesn't put food on our table or clothes on our backs. What am I going to do with you, Benny? I can barely make ends meet as it is. With you for a helper, we'll all end up in the poorhouse."

"Pop, I'll make it up to you. Really, I will. I'll find a way."

"What way? Running out to throw a baseball around in the backyard like you did last week when you were supposed to be watching the store while I made deliveries? Is that how?"

"Pop, I . . ."

"Get out of here, Benny. Clean that mess up and get out of here."

"But Pop . . ."

"I don't need you, Benny." He turned and walked back into the store.

I felt tears at the back of my eyes, but I didn't let them out. I didn't want Henry to see me cry, even if he was my friend. I wet some rags at the sink in the little bathroom and then knelt down to wipe up the sticky goop. Henry was carefully picking out the salvageable eggs and putting them in an empty crate. "At least," he said, "you can come out and play now. I can throw some for you, or we can go down by the river and mess around."

"You don't know anything about it," I said angrily. I felt so guilty I could hardly stand it. My father was a round, gentle man. He never yelled. He hadn't even yelled this time over a whole crate of ruined eggs. And he certainly never hit me. He had never hit any of us. But sometimes I thought I would feel better if my father did yell at me, or spank me. My mother yelled or slapped pretty regularly. And when she was done yelling, she was done being angry. But my father just kept looking sad. There seemed to be no end to the sadness in his soft brown eyes. Sometimes I felt so guilty when I looked into those nearsighted eyes behind their wire-rimmed glasses that I didn't know what to do. I felt guilty just for being me—not smart, like Sheldon, not good, like Evelyn. Just dumb, clumsy Benny.

Henry had enough sense to keep his mouth shut while we finished cleaning up. When we were done, we walked out together into the yard. The sun shone. It was a glorious day. Really, I couldn't stay miserable very long on such an unusual occasion— a warm April Saturday on which I had been granted complete and total freedom. I usually did have part of the afternoon off on a Saturday, but today I'd been let out earlier than usual because Pop was too annoyed with me to want me around. Well, I was sorry he was mad, but I was glad to be free.

"Pitch a few to me, Henry," I said. Henry picked up the bat, ball, and glove which he had dropped next to the back door before coming in. The yard was too small now for me to hit the ball in it. It had been good enough the previous year, but this spring, since I'd grown so much, I had found that I was constantly hitting out of my own yard and into the ones on either side. The people who owned those stores weren't too happy about that. The street was too busy for playing ball. The next one over, where Henry lived, had a couple of empty lots. We walked over to one of them, and Henry threw balls to me while I hit them. I hit every one of them. The lot was pretty small, too, and I kept hitting into the street or an adjoining yard. We spent too much time chasing the balls, and I got tired of it. Finally I said to Henry, "It's your turn now. I'll pitch and you hit a few."

"Nope," Henry replied firmly. "I told you we were all through with that taking turns business. We're not going to waste any time on that. I'm training you."

"But we always used to take turns," I insisted. "It was better then."

"No, it wasn't." Henry shook his head grimly. "This is our chance," he said. "You know that. We're going to get back at all those guys who never

21

pick us for the team. One of these days they're going to be short a guy and they're going to have to
pick you, and will they ever be surprised! It'll be
the best day of my life."

"You're dreaming, Henry. It'll never happen.
They'll never pick us."

"Not us," Henry reminded me. "Just you. You're
the one who got so big and powerful this year.
You're like a bear who hibernates in a cave all
winter. But in the spring you came out bigger instead of smaller. And all put together too."

"Yeah?" I asked sarcastically. "Then why do I
drop egg crates?"

"I don't care about the grocery store," Henry
said, waving his hand at me. "I care about the
ball field!"

"Well," I said, "since no one has noticed this big
change in me but you, fat chance I'll ever even get
into a ball game."

"Keep practicing," Henry said. "Mac and his guys
don't hate you. One day they'll ask you."

"No," I said, "they don't hate me. They just don't
know I exist."

"I read about it in *Liberty* magazine," Henry
said. He didn't wait for an answer. "You got an
inferiority complex." Henry read a lot of books and
stuff. Half the time I didn't even know what he was
talking about.

"What's that?" I asked.

"I read about it in *Liberty* magazine," Henry said. "It means you don't think you're any good. The article said you have to like yourself before anyone else can like you." Imagine Henry reading *Liberty* magazine. All I ever read was the sports page of the newspaper and comic books about this guy called Superman. Henry read them too. He gave them to me after he was done.

"Well," I said, "if you really aren't any good and that's what you think, then you're just thinking the truth. I don't see what's wrong with that."

"I give up," Henry said. "You don't understand anything."

"That's what I mean," I said.

"Conversation with you is a waste," Henry said. "Hitting balls is better. Let's go to the park. There you'll have all the room you need."

"No," I said. "I've had enough baseball for now. Let's go to the river."

"O.K.," Henry agreed. "No one's home at my house. We'll go in and make some peanut butter sandwiches and take 'em with us."

"O.K.," I said.

three

The river was lined with textile mills ceaselessly spewing out colored water, sometimes blue, sometimes green, but usually a nauseous yellow-brown. The river wasn't good for swimming and hadn't been since years before I had even been born. But it was water, and there's always something to do by the water.

Sometimes we fished. We never caught anything but an occasional inedible spiny catfish. The river wasn't much friendlier to marine life than it was to people. Now and then, though, we pulled out some interesting garbage—rubber tires, a waterlogged jacket, wooden crates. We had heard about one boy, just about twelve, like us, who tangled his line around the half-sunken corpse of a murdered man.

That day, though, we didn't fish. We sat on the wreck of an old rowboat beached in the long grass that grew on the muddy banks and ate our peanut butter sandwiches, watching an endless procession of boats going by, mostly barges loaded with textiles, oil, coal, or machinery. The barges moved very slowly and there was plenty of time for us to get to know their crews by waving and hollering. Sometimes smaller boats sailed close enough to the shore so we could actually talk to the men on board.

"Where ya bound for?"

"Newark."

"What're you carrying?"

"Barrels."

"Barrels of what?"

"Just barrels."

I liked the river. It was a separate world, a dream world, even if it was dirty. "You know," I said to Henry, "I'd like to get on one of those barges and take a ride to Newark. It'd be a lot more fun going to visit my aunt on a boat than taking the streetcar. You ever been on a boat?"

Henry shook his head. "Nope." Then he added, "What d'ya take the streetcar to Newark for? Why don't you go in your father's delivery truck?"

"We used to," I explained, "but there's only room

for Ma and Pop and Evvie in the front. So Sheldon and me got to ride in the back, and Sheldon won't do that anymore. He's such a big man nowadays he can't ride in the back of a truck. The old thing's going to fall apart any minute anyhow. We got it three years ago and it was six years old then. If it dies, Pop says we're really in trouble. The only reason he's been able to stay in business since the new A&P came in is because he takes orders over the phone and delivers."

"Yeah," Henry agreed. "My old man says things are real tough all over still. He says we haven't seen the last of this depression yet, no matter what Roosevelt says. Of course, he's got more money than God, but he likes to pretend he doesn't. Your old man may be kind of poor, but at least he isn't mean, like mine."

I didn't like being called poor, not even by Henry. "We're not really poor," I insisted. "There's always enough. I always get movie and ice cream money every week. They just worry all the time, that's all. They're just always worried."

"Except Sheldon," Henry said. "Sheldon's almost as mean as my old man."

"Oh, Sheldon worries," I said. "He worries about passing that test to get into Cooper Union. If he gets in, he gets a free education. He gets to be an engineer for nothing. That's why he's got to spend all his time studying, and I've got to spend all my time helping in the store. He never takes a turn anymore watching the store while Pop's making deliveries."

"My God," Henry said. "Sheldon'll pass that test in a walk. He's the biggest genius in the county—maybe in the whole state of New Jersey. Everyone knows that."

"Yeah," I replied gloomily. "You know that and I know that, but Sheldon doesn't know that. He's convinced he's got to study every single second he's not at school between now and that test next month, and he's convinced my mom and pop too."

"Sheldon is a jerk," Henry said.

I didn't much like Henry's saying that, either. Still, I said it all the time myself, so I couldn't very well disagree. "Sheldon worries just like the rest of our family," I explained. "It's just that he worries about different things."

Henry picked up an empty beer bottle and threw it in the river. I picked up an empty Coke bottle and did the same. My bottle landed much farther out in the river than Henry's. For a while we threw bits of the garbage that littered the bank into the river. My missiles always landed much farther out than Henry's, though Henry was huffing and puffing with the effort to throw as far as he could and I didn't even have to try. Last fall, sometimes my old stick or beer bottle went farther, sometimes Henry's. This spring it was always mine.

27

After we'd used up the junk we could reach without leaving our spot, we threw our own sandwich wrappings into the river and watched them float toward Newark with the current. I wondered if they'd make it all the way, or if they'd get waterlogged somewhere around Belleville and sink to the bottom. One day I'd put a message in a bottle and send it down the river. Maybe some kid down by Newark would find it and write me a letter. I'd never gotten a letter.

Then we walked over to the bridge. It was a very unusual bridge, and we loved watching it work. Most of the barges that sailed the river were low and passed under the bridge easily. But sometimes a ship with high smokestacks or an upper deck came down the river, and then the bridge had to move. Most of the bridges farther up the river were drawbridges. The road simply parted and the halves were drawn up in the air by an elaborate system of weights and balances to allow tall ships to pass through. But this bridge did something different. Its roadbed rotated ninety degrees so that instead of running across the river, it was parallel to it. Then the ships could pass on either side of it.

We walked up on the bridge. It had sidewalks, but that afternoon there were no other walkers. Cars and trucks sped by us at a steady clip, but we didn't pay any attention to them. Instead, we leaned over the railing and watched the traffic on the river below. The view was really different from the one we'd had on the bank.

After a while, I didn't hear sounds of traffic behind me anymore. I turned and saw that the bridge was empty of cars and trucks. Approaching it from downriver was a big ship with two decks. The bridge engineer was leaning out of the window of his little house on the other side of the bridge screaming at us. "Get off the bridge, you kids," he shouted. "Get off the bridge."

Henry started to run. "Come on, Benny," he said. "Let's get out of here. This bridge is going to move."

I grabbed him by the shirttail. "Let's stay," I said. "Let's take a ride!"

Henry stared at me. "You crazy? We could get killed."

"You're a dope," I answered. "It's safer than riding a streetcar. Besides, it's too late now!"

It was too late. The bridge engineer had given up on us. He had set the machinery in motion. Slowly, with smooth and graceful dignity, the bridge was beginning to move. Clutching the rail, I watched the river slide away beneath me, and the Occidental Silk Mill on the bank draw closer and closer. Then the bridge stopped moving, and the great ship sailed by, almost close enough to touch. Henry and I waved violently to the men on the deck and they waved back. When the ship had traveled the length of the bridge, the bridge majestically began its journey back into place. I sat on the middle rail, with my arm around the upper one, and felt as if I were gliding slowly through the air. Henry kept his feet planted firmly on the sidewalk.

With a great creak, the bridge snapped into place. I hopped off the rail and we started running toward our end of the bridge—luckily the one opposite the bridge engineer. We didn't want to tangle with him. He leaned out of his window and shouted, "Crazy kids. Don't ever let me catch you on this bridge again!" He had more to say, but we didn't even hear it. By the time we got to the end of the bridge we were too far away to hear anything shouted from the other side.

"Wasn't that great? Wasn't that the greatest?" I said as I fell into the grass. "The only thing that could be better would be to sail in that ship itself, or maybe to fly in an airplane."

"It was O.K.," Henry said. "It made me a little nervous."

"Not me," I said. "I wasn't worried at all. You know, nobody can get to you out there. When you're on that bridge turning around, you're really free. Even the bridge man couldn't get to us."

"What'll we do now?" Henry asked. "Now would be a good time to go to the park."

I didn't really hear him. In my mind I was still

moving slowly above the river, like a sea gull. Henry shoved me. "Hey, Benny, listen to me. Let's go to the park. Maybe Mac and the other guys'll be there now, playing ball. Maybe they'll let us in the game."

"Stop dreaming," I said. "You know they won't. Besides, I gotta get back to the store. Soon it'll be time for my father to make deliveries."

"You heard what he said," Henry reminded me. "He said he didn't need you."

"But he didn't mean it." I knew that if I didn't show up when my father had to go out to make deliveries, I'd feel even worse than I had over the broken eggs. I hadn't been free for very long. But I could remember it. I could remember that high, cool joy I had felt as I had floated slowly over the river so far below.

————four————

The next day our whole family went on the street-car to Newark to visit Aunt Goldie and Uncle Moe. My father closed the store Sundays, though my grandfather had worked seven days a week. But Pop said since there was no chance he was ever going to get rich anyway, he might as well have one day to spend with his wife and children. Sheldon hadn't wanted to come. He said he had to stay home and study. But Pop had insisted. "If I can take a day off, so can you." So Sheldon had come. Ma carried a large brown paper bag on her lap, containing a pan of noodle pudding wrapped in wax paper. She had gotten up early to make it. Evelyn was really annoyed when she had come into the kitchen to start breakfast and found Ma already there.

"Get back to bed, Ma," she said. "I'll fix breakfast."

"I won't go to Goldie's empty-handed," Ma had replied.

"I can make a noodle pudding," Evelyn said.

"No you can't," Ma said. "Not a *real* noodle pudding."

"You'll be exhausted all day if you do this," Evvie pointed out. "You won't enjoy the visit."

"I'll rest after I get it in the oven. What's going to happen here, I'm going to be an invalid forever, never do a thing in my own house?"

Evvie didn't say anything more. She just made breakfast and cleaned up and got herself dressed and told me to put on a clean shirt and my good knickers.

On the way to Goldie and Moe's house, we talked. The Teitelbaums had been over to play gin rummy with Ma and Pop the night before, so Sheldon hadn't had much chance to talk about the egg-dropping incident. He wasn't about to let it go by.

"If I'd done something like that," he said to Pop, "you'd have mortalized me. But you didn't do a thing to Benny to punish him. Not a thing."

"What did you want me to do?" Pop replied mildly. "Did you want me to beat him to a pulp? Would that have satisfied you?"

"Benny is your precious little baby," Sheldon announced. "We can't punish our precious little baby, can we?"

"Benny used to be delicate," Ma said dreamily, her eyes focused on some distant scene in the past. "When he was two, he got scarlet fever. I nursed him day and night, till I got sick myself. Oh, I was so proud when he started to gain weight again."

"And he hasn't stopped since," Sheldon said. "That scarlet fever sure didn't affect his body any, but maybe it affected his brain."

Ma nodded solemnly. "Maybe it did," she agreed.

"Don't be ridiculous," Pa said.

"Well," Sheldon said, "you gotta stop babying Benny. I'm saying this for his own sake. You gotta treat him like a grown-up, and when he does wrong, you gotta punish him, or he'll never get to be a man."

I didn't entirely disagree with Sheldon. I just looked at things a little different from the way he did. I didn't think they spoiled me at all. I thought they asked an awful lot of me. But they treated me like a baby all right. They took good care of me, just like they had when I had had scarlet fever, but they didn't know anything about me, and they weren't making any effort to find out.

Well, Goldie made an effort. Goldie knew about me. I was glad to be going to her house. We all were. Goldie and Moe had two teen-aged daughters still at home and all the kids in their neighborhood were always in their sun parlor or on their front porch. Goldie herself was like a magnet. She had been elected president of five different organizations within two years of joining them. First she had been president of the Lublin Landsleit of Newark, then of the Hebrew Ladies Aid Society, then of the Chancellor Avenue School PTA, then of the Hebrew School committee at her local synagogue, and currently of the Weequahic Chapter of Hadassah. She was certainly the only president the Chancellor Avenue School PTA had ever had who spoke with a thick Yiddish accent. She was intelligent and kind, but I don't think that's why she got elected to everything. I think she got chosen because she had the best sense of humor in Essex County and attending a meeting she was running was as good as listening to Fred Allen on the radio. Though she was only a few years older than my father, she was actually his aunt, his dead mother's youngest sister, so we visited her as often as we visited Grandma and Grandpa Goldfarb, more often really, because we liked her better.

She stood on the front porch of her house to greet us. She was a short, plump, gray-haired, homely woman, and her legs were bowed because she had bad arthritis. She was practically a cripple and had to walk like a duck, but that didn't seem to stop her from doing anything she wanted to do.

She kissed and hugged us all as if she hadn't seen us in a year and a half. "Sick as you are, Gertie, you made a noodle pudding? You put me to shame." Ma smiled, for the first time since she'd come home from the hospital four weeks before. "Jake, Moe is waiting for you in the living room by the radio. He's listening to President Roosevelt opening the World's Fair while he reads *The News of the Week in Review*." Pop hurried in to join Moe, the only person he knew who took what was happening in Europe seriously enough to satisfy him. "Evvie, the girls are in the sun parlor. God knows who else. Sheldon, you can go with her. Even Einstein rests his brain. The violin you can't play, but you can try the victrola." To me she gave a special warm hug and kiss. I felt I was too old for kisses from female relatives, but I hadn't found a way of telling this to Aunt Goldie, and besides, I wasn't really sure I wanted to. "How's my boy?" she asked. "My God, you're going to be taller than Moe even. Like a regular Cossack you're going to be. What've you been up to this week?"

"He dropped a whole crate of eggs," Sheldon said. "Inside that hulk he's got a brain the size of a pea."

"The girls in the sun parlor," Goldie repeated,

looking straight at Sheldon. "Boys too. Arthur Brabant just won a full scholarship to Columbia. Go in and talk to him. You'll find out maybe he's even smarter than you." Sheldon went.

Evvie put the noodle pudding in the kitchen before joining the gang in the sun parlor. Ma, Aunt Goldie, and I sat down on the porch.

"Nu, Gertie, how're you feeling?" Goldie inquired sympathetically.

"Oy, Goldie, it's taking me so long to get better. Sometimes I think I never will."

"Don't worry, darling, everyone gets better from a hysterectomy."

"But I have so many things to worry about. If I didn't worry all the time, I'd get better faster."

"What do you have to worry about?"

"Sheldon. Will Sheldon pass his test?"

"Will Sheldon pass his test? Will Babe Ruth hit a home run?"

"Times are bad."

"They've been bad for ten years. For all of us. They're getting better."

"I don't like the boy Evvie's going around with."

"Evvie's only sixteen. She isn't marrying him."

"I started going with Jake when I was thirteen."

"And if she does marry him, what's so terrible? Morty Katz is a nice boy."

"From a poor family."

"So's she."

"What am I going to do with Benny? He doesn't get good marks in school like the others. He breaks everything he touches. All he wants to do is hang around empty lots playing baseball with that Henry Silverberg."

Goldie turned to me. "Is that all you like to do, Benny?" she asked seriously. "Is that all, really?"

"Well, not all," I answered just as seriously. "There are a couple of other things I like to do. I like to sing and whistle. I like to throw stones in the river and watch the boats. Yesterday I took a ride on the bridge. I sure liked that."

"You what?" my mother almost shrieked.

I hadn't meant to tell anyone about that ride. But I couldn't help telling Goldie. I started to explain. "Yesterday. Henry and me. It began to move."

"You could have been killed," my mother cried. She turned to Goldie. "Do you see what I mean?"

"It was swell," I insisted. "It was the best thing. We couldn't have gotten killed. There was no way. Unless we fell off. It's no easier to fall off that bridge when it's moving than when it's still." I didn't bother to mention that I had sat on the rail during the trip.

"Benny, that wasn't smart," my mother said. "You're just not smart and one of these days you're going to get killed!"

"Smart. Smart. What good is smart?" Goldie asked. "So I'm smart, Benny, right? Everyone says I'm smart."

I nodded.

"So listen to what your smart Aunt Goldie did. Just listen. Since Millie got married, her room's been empty. Essie talks about moving in there, but she never gets around to it. So one day I'm talking to my friend, Mrs. Kossoff. Some friend. She tells me she doesn't sleep any more with Mr. Kossoff. After her son got that job in Chicago, Mr. Kossoff moved into Jerry's room. 'Goldie,' she says to me, 'such good rest I get now. Every night. At our age what we need is a good rest. With your arthritis, you should be sleeping in your own bed.'"

"Goldie," Ma said warningly, glancing over at me. "Don't forget *das kind*." Why she thought I wouldn't understand her if she said *the child* in Yiddish, I'll never know.

Goldie paid no attention to her. She was telling her story to me. "For a smart woman, I'm dumb. I listen to Mrs. Kossoff. Why? I don't know why. So I say to Moe, 'Moe, we're getting old. We need our rest. We should sleep in separate rooms.'

"So Moe says to me, 'Goldie,' he says, 'I've slept in the same bed for thirty years. I'm not moving now. You don't like it, you move.' So I moved. I moved into Millie's room. Where, according to Mrs. Kossoff, the expert, I'm supposed to sleep better. Let me tell you, better I didn't sleep. I didn't shut my eyes for a whole week. For thirty years I slept with him, how the devil am I supposed to sleep without him? I missed him! But I couldn't tell him that. After all, I'm supposed to be the smart one. It looked like I was going to spend the rest of my nights with my eyes open!"

"Like me," Ma interrupted. "I never sleep a wink. Never."

"So what'd you do?" I asked, fascinated. "How did you get out of it?"

"That's the point, Benny," Goldie said admiringly. "That's exactly the point. Everybody makes mistakes. What's important is how you get out of them. I call up another friend—a real one, this time—Minna Baumann. You know her. She runs a boarding house over on Peshine Avenue. I said if she was all filled up and she knew a nice young man who needed a room, send him over. In two days a man came. I rented him the room for five dollars a week and moved back in with Moe. So now I can sleep and I'm five dollars richer each week too!"

"Where is he?" I asked. "I want to meet him."

"Oh, he goes home to Scranton, Pennsylvania, on weekends to see his family. He won't be back till late tonight. Actually, I got to figure out a way to get rid of him now. This is a small house. I really don't need a stranger. Maybe he'll decide Newark, New Jersey, is no place for a nice boy from the country."

I laughed. "The important thing," I repeated, "is not that you made a mistake. The important thing is how you got out of it."

"The first time, anyway," Goldie said. "If you make the same mistake twice, then you *are* dumb."

"Your house isn't small," Ma said. "It's a lot bigger than ours. Five dollars a week. That's nothing to sneeze at."

Somehow Ma had missed the point. But I didn't tell her. Goldie went to the kitchen to get dinner and Ma went with her to do what she could while sitting at the kitchen table, like shelling peas or cutting celery. I went into the sun parlor and sat on the day bed while Essie, Sylvia, Sheldon, Arthur Brabant, and Evvie played records on the victrola, flirted, and talked about people I'd never met.

I didn't find any of it very interesting until the subject of the World's Fair came up. They all agreed they wanted to get there as soon as they could. They weren't very definite about the date because if one of them was free on a certain day, another was not. But Sylvia ran into the living room to get the special section of *The New York Times* devoted that day to the fair, and they pored over the maps.

"The place to start," Arthur Brabant said, "is the Trylon and the Perisphere. Then you can kind of work your way out in circles."

"That's a stupid plan," Sheldon said, "because they're nowhere near the entrance. What're you going to do? Shut your eyes so you won't see anything else on your way over to them?"

41

I looked over Sheldon's shoulder at the picture of the Trylon. It was a tall, pointy thing. "Can you go up in that Trylon?" I asked. "Can you go up in it and look out over the whole fair for miles and miles?"

"No," Arthur said. "It has no windows."

I was disappointed. Then Evvie said, "I bet you'd like this one, though, Benny." She grabbed the paper out of Sheldon's hands and turned to the descriptions of specific exhibits. "Here," she said. "General Motors, World of Tomorrow." She handed me the paper, pointing, and I read aloud, ". . . a huge diorama designed by Norman Bel Geddes to show hundreds of miles of American scenery, complete with cities and towns, rivers and lakes, mountains, forests, farmlands, with moving traffic and smoking factories. Visitors, in moving chairs with sound equipment to explain the trip, tour this scene and emerge at the full-size intersection with a feeling that they have really arrived in the future."

"That sounds good," Essie said. "I'd really like to see that."

"Good?" I echoed. "Good? It sounds great. It sounds like the greatest thing I ever heard of. It must be like riding in an airplane with everything real little down below you, only instead of riding through space, you're riding through time too."

"Oh, Benny, you don't know what you're talking about," Sheldon said. "How do you know what it's like? You've never even seen it, and you probably never will."

"Come on, Sheldon," Essie said. "No one's seen it because the fair is only opening today. His idea of it sounds pretty good to me. And I bet he does see it, too. The fair's going to be there for two summers, so we all ought to get to see it sooner or later."

Sylvia had lost interest in the conversation and was now at the old upright piano playing "Smoke Gets in Your Eyes," the only song she knew. The others joined her, leaving me alone in the corner with the special section. Until they called me in for dinner, I wasn't bored at all. I examined every map and picture, and I read every word, from cover to cover.

five

Monday morning my father woke me up very early. He shook me gently so that he wouldn't disturb Sheldon. I got dressed quickly and then went downstairs to help him unload the crates of fruits and vegetables he had picked up at the wholesale market in Newark at five o'clock in the morning. Three times a week he went into the wholesale market before the sun was up, and three times a week I helped him unload the truck before I went to school.

I barely had time to gulp down a glass of milk

44

and a piece of rye bread and butter before Henry was yelling for me from the bottom of the stairs. It was a good thing the entire household was awake by the time Henry came, because nothing anyone said to him ever stopped him from standing at the foot of the stairs, right inside the door, and screaming, "Ben-eee. Ben-eee. Let's go-o-o." When Ma had first come home from the hospital, Evelyn had suggested that perhaps Henry wouldn't mind coming up the stairs for the next few days when he came to get me. Henry said he wouldn't mind, but he never did it.

I grabbed my books and ran out of the kitchen. "Don't fool around on your way home," Ma called after me. Then she said to Evvie, "One day last week he didn't get to the store until nearly four o'clock!"

I didn't hear Evvie's answer. I was out the door and halfway down the stairs by the time she had a chance to say anything. I was lucky Sheldon had already left.

We got to school nearly half an hour before the bell rang. We always got to school early. I didn't like the inside of school, but I liked the outside. Everything important went on in the school yard.

We leaned up against the fence and watched the action. We put our hands inside our knicker pockets and made our faces as still and expressionless as masks. We didn't stand in the best spot, opposite the entrance labeled *Girls,* a label that had had no meaning for at least ten years. I didn't know why the choice leaning spot was against the fence opposite that door. Neither did anyone else. But it had been that way as long as anyone at Albert Payson Terhune Elementary School could remember.

Henry and I stood well down from the point of honor, and we stood alone. Facing the door directly was Mac. His eyes scanned the playground rapidly. Otherwise his face showed no movement, no emotion. His buddies surrounded him—Carlo, Willy Matthews, Double Dip Cohen, and the others who played ball with him during recess and after school.

Nancy Stein and her formation of eighth-grade girls came careening around the corner of the building, as they did two or three times a week. They were all tall, with heavy thighs under their cotton dresses, and they ran across the yard with their arms linked, headed right for a group of third-grade boys shooting marbles in the middle of the playground. The boys surrounding the shooters saw them coming and a few of them managed to scatter. But the two boys on the ground didn't have a chance, and those in the gallery who hadn't moved fast enough got it too. Three of them were laid flat out on the ground and two others barely escaped as the screaming line roared through their playing area.

It was really sad to watch the little boys pick

themselves up, brush themselves off, and fight to hold back their tears. One of them began scrambling for the scattered marbles and another shouted to the girls, who stood around laughing, their line now broken, "You dirty rats. You dumb dirty rats."

"How long has Nancy Stein and her gang been doing that?" I asked.

"Ever since we were in kindergarten," Henry answered. "She used to do it to us."

"For as long as she could," I remembered. "But we're only two years smaller than she is. She really didn't get good at it until last year, when she moved over to the other playground." The seventh and eighth graders hung out on the playground on their side of the building, where the entrance was labeled *Boys*. The sixth graders were the biggest kids on the *Girls* side.

"Shut your mouth, kid, or you'll get it again," Nancy Stein shouted at the third grader who had had the nerve to talk back to her. She and the largest of her gang, Agnes Delanoy, were advancing on the little boy with blood in their eyes.

Suddenly there was movement along the fence. Mac had taken two steps away from his position. His hands were out of his pockets. Carlo, Willy, and Double Dip followed behind him.

"Come on," Henry said to me. We stepped out behind Double Dip.

Double Dip turned and gave us a cold stare.

47

"Mac," he said. Mac turned too, briefly, shook his head, and then moved on.

We moved back against the fence. I felt like the third-grade marble shooter who had rubbed the tears out of his eyes. But I kept my hands in my pockets where they belonged.

Mac and his gang moved without haste but steady as the Lackawanna Railroad until they formed a line behind Nancy Stein and Agnes Delanoy. They were now between the two ringleaders and the other girls. The brave third grader had retreated, but he had not turned his back on Nancy and Agnes.

"Take it back, kid," Nancy said. "Take back what you called us."

"You *are* dirty rats," the boy said. "Mickey and Paul lost all their best marbles."

"You bet they lost their marbles," Agnes laughed. "They never had any to begin with."

"Paul had an aggie cost him a quarter. You dirty rats," he added defiantly.

The girls took a step forward. "O.K.," Mac said. "O.K., kid. That's enough."

The third grader looked at Mac. Mac smiled. The boy moved back among his friends, who were standing in a crooked semicircle, watching. Nancy turned to Mac. "O.K., you called him off. But I won't take talk like that next time."

"There ain't gonna be no next time," Mac said.

"You stay on your own playground from now on. Pick on kids your own size."

"Who's gonna make us?" Agnes sneered.

"We are," Mac said quietly.

"You'd hit a girl?" Nancy asked.

"Not most girls," Carlo said. "We wouldn't hit Mary Higgins. We wouldn't hit Elena Martinelli. Would we, Mac?"

"No, we wouldn't," Mac said. Carlo and Mac were facing Nancy and Agnes. Willy and Double Dip had turned around and were looking at the six other girls who made up Nancy's line. The rest of Mac's gang stood behind them, against the fence, their arms loose at their sides, their palms open. A little space away from them, Henry and I also leaned against the fence in silence, staring at the encounter in front of us. An uncanny quiet had fallen over the playground. I couldn't remember its ever having been so quiet. I had no trouble at all hearing the sounds of traffic out on Bond Street, but they seemed very far away, like noises from another world.

Nancy broke the silence. "Aw, hell," she said. "What do we want with little jerks like you?" She walked away. Agnes and the others followed her. In twenty seconds they had disappeared around the side of the building.

Suddenly the playground was filled with noise again. Everyone was talking, yelling, screaming, shouting, running, jumping, hopping, and skipping. Even Mac and his boys stood in the middle of the playground, in a knot, talking to each other, and smiling.

When the bell rang, we lined up in rows by class outside the door. The sixth graders went in last, Mrs. Elfand's class on the left, Miss O'Connor's class on the right. We lined up, as always, in size order. I was at the end of the line; Mac was right in front of me.

We were supposed to shut up as soon as we got in line, but today we couldn't, even though Miss Hortatis, the teacher monitor for the week, had already opened the door.

"That was something, Mac," I whispered to him. "That was really something. You fixed her. She'll never bother us again."

"She better not," Mac said, "if she knows what's good for her."

Mac was really talkative that morning. Those ten words were more than he had ever said to me before in the six months he'd been at Terhune. Not that he ever picked on me, or made nasty cracks when I gave wrong answers in class. Mac wasn't like Willy Matthews. It was just that he didn't notice me at all. To a guy like Mac, guys like me didn't even exist.

Mac had shown up in Mrs. Elfand's sixth grade in the middle of October, and by Halloween everyone knew he was boss of the class. He was big and smart and a fantastic athlete. More than anything else, everyone wanted to be his friend. Me too, of course. But Mac had been busy with Willy Matthews, Double Dip Cohen, Fred LaPorta, and even Carlo, who was very small but shrewd and funny as a monkey. There was no chance he'd even look at someone like me.

I didn't hold that against him. Willy had been the boss of Mrs. Elfand's sixth grade before Mac came and Mac was a big improvement. He didn't say any more to me as we walked into the classroom, and I didn't say any more to him. I wasn't about to press my luck.

The morning passed very slowly. It always passed very slowly. Sometimes Mrs. Elfand asked a question I knew I could answer if I wanted to, but I never wanted to. Suppose I answered wrong?

I didn't hate Mrs. Elfand. She was strict, but very fair. She loved music, so with her we had singing every day, not just once a week when the music teacher came. I liked to sing. Of course, I had never told anyone that, except Goldie. We were supposed to hate singing, and the other guys griped about having to perform "The Happy Wanderer" and "La Paloma" every day of the week. But they sang. Mrs. Elfand didn't tolerate closed mouths during singing any more than she tolerated open ones during work periods. I sang loudest of all. Fortunately,

51

since I was so tall, I sat in the back of the room, where no one was likely to notice how loud I sang. No one, that is, except Mrs. Elfand. She noticed and wanted to give me a solo in the Christmas concert, but I had to turn her down. My folks weren't the most observant Jews in the world, but they would have had a heart attack if they'd heard me singing "O Holy Night" all alone in front of three hundred people.

First thing in the morning, though, we didn't have music. We had arithmetic.

"Benny, will you please put the seventh problem in the arithmetic homework on the board?" Mrs. Elfand's voice shattered my pleasant dream in which I was delivering a solo rendition of "The Road to Mandalay" at the spring concert. I looked down at my arithmetic book. The page to which I had opened it didn't even have any problems on it, let alone a problem number seven.

A crumpled piece of arithmetic paper stuck out beyond the pages of the book. I turned to that page and saw the homework problems I had tried to work. They involved mixed fractions. I had not gotten as far as number seven.

"Benny," Mrs. Elfand repeated firmly, "come up to the board, *now,* please."

I walked slowly to the board, trying to read the problem as I went. "John buys 8 marbles at 3/4 of a penny each." How ridiculous. Who ever heard of a marble that cost 3/4 of a cent? Two for a penny, maybe, if they were really crummy marbles, but not any figure as silly as 3/4 of a cent each. "How much did John pay for 8 marbles?"

In a flash, I thought, "Six cents." If you took three quarters and added it up eight times, you were going to get something like six. But that couldn't be the right answer, and besides, I had no idea how I'd gotten it. Mrs. Elfand didn't just want answers, wrong or right. She wanted to see the work.

On the board I wrote, "3/4 × 8." Then I erased the 8 and wrote "1/8." Then I wrote "= 3/32." But what was I supposed to do next? I didn't know how to divide 3 by 32. Could you divide 3 by 32? Probably not. Three apples divided into 32 parts was applesauce. Three divided by 32 certainly wasn't 6. I ought to write something down, anything, but whatever I wrote, it surely would be wrong, so it would be better to write down nothing. I stared at the board for a minute and then put the chalk down on the rail.

"All right, Benny," Mrs. Elfand said at last. "You may sit down. Stay after school and I'll give you some extra help on these problems."

"I can't stay after scohol, Mrs. Elfand," I replied. "I have to help my father in the store."

"Perhaps *he* can help you with these problems," Mrs. Elfand suggested. "Or maybe your brother." Mrs. Elfand had taught Sheldon six years ago and she hadn't forgotten him. No teacher ever did.

Sheldon wouldn't save me if I were drowning,

let alone help me with my homework. But out loud I said only, "Yes, ma'am."

"You want to go on to seventh grade, don't you?" Mrs. Elfand asked.

"Yes, ma'am."

"Then you'd better do something about your work, and quickly," she said.

"Yes, ma'am." The threat of staying back. It had lurked in the background every year I'd been in school, but this was the first time it had ever been mentioned openly. If my parents heard about it they would die. It would be a million times worse for them than my singing "O Holy Night" in the Christmas concert.

"If I call your father and tell him how serious the problem is, maybe he'll excuse you from working in the store and let you stay after school for extra help."

"Don't do that," I said desperately. "Not yet. I'll try very hard from now on." The palms of my hands had begun to sweat.

"See that you do," Mrs. Elfand said severely. "Go ahead. Sit down now."

I walked back to my seat. "Dummy," Willy Matthews whispered at me, without even turning his head. "Dummy." Mrs. Elfand heard the whisper, but she didn't know where it came from, and Mrs. Elfand never made an issue of what she could not do anything about. She called on Carlo. He went to the board and wrote "3/4 × 8/1 = 24/4 = 6."

So 6 *was* the right answer. I should have known.

Mrs. Elfand left me alone for the rest of the arithmetic lesson. I tried to concentrate on the work, but it was hard. Sometimes I thought I was back on the bridge, swinging through the air like a bird. I couldn't wait to try that again. But of course the bridge engineer would never let me. He'd be on the lookout for us for months to come.

After arithmetic we had reading. That was a little better. I was in the slowest reading group, but I was not the slowest reader in the slowest group. I might have practiced reading more if they gave me things to read like the *Times* World's Fair section, things that weren't so boring. Later on I found out there were books just as good as Superman comics. Even better. But I was old by then.

After reading came social studies, and then lunch, thank God. Lunch and recess.

six

Henry and I went out into the schoolyard and took our usual position against the fence, slowly chewing on our apples and sandwiches. Henry had peanut butter and jelly, but I had peanut butter and slices of canned pineapple. Evvie was very imaginative.

Mac, Willy, Carlo, and the rest of their gang ate quickly, so they could start playing baseball as soon as possible.

"Move down a little," Henry told me.

"Why?" Henry was at it again, trying to get us noticed.

"So we can see their game better," he replied.

"You think maybe if we're down there closer to them maybe they'll ask us to play? Forget it. They won't."

"Abie Zaretski is absent today. Maybe they'll want someone to fill in."

"They're not playing a real game. There isn't enough room here anyway. They're just practicing. The real game is this afternoon, after school."

"I know all that," Henry interrupted. "So what?"

"So now they don't care how many they got. It doesn't matter. They're not gonna ask us to play."

"Let's move down anyway," Henry insisted.

So we moved down. After all, it was a free fence.

Mac's gang had cleared all the other kids out of the section of the schoolyard beyond the building. There wasn't enough room to lay out a regulation-sized diamond, but there was enough room to practice.

Carlo pitched a ball to Mac. Mac hit the ball straight to Willy at second base. Then he slammed the tip of his bat to the ground. You could see he was mad. "How the hell are we ever gonna beat those guys from Hamilton School this afternoon without someone who can really hit 'em?"

"You can really hit," Fred LaPorta comforted Mac. Fred was the catcher. "You're just off a little today."

"Oh, I can hit 'em, I guess," Mac said. "And I'm a darn good pitcher. You guys are pretty good hit-ters too—you and Double Dip and Carlo. But not one of us is what you'd call a real slugger. We need a slugger."

Mrs. Elfand came over to the fence where Henry and I were standing. She was playground monitor that week. Since there were twenty teachers, and only two of them had to be playground monitors at a time, Mrs. Elfand hadn't been out on the playground at all since baseball season had begun.

"Don't you want to play ball?" she asked us.

"Nope," I said, as casually as I could. I didn't even take my hands out of my pockets. "We don't . . . we don't feel much like playing today."

Mrs. Elfand lifted her eyebrows and looked me right in the eye. I turned away from her glance, staring intently at Mac as he pitched a ball to Double Dip. "What about you?" she asked Henry. "Don't you 'feel like' playing either?"

"Yeah," said Henry. "I feel like playing. So does Benny. But they don't want to play with us. They never do. Even if we bring a new ball and a glove and everything, they won't play with us. It isn't fair." Henry was the best reader in the class. He liked Mrs. Elfand and she liked him. He wasn't afraid to tell her what he really felt, so long as she was asking. But to me at that moment he seemed like a traitor.

I grabbed his shoulder. "Don't push it," I said through gritted teeth. "Don't push it."

58

But it was too late. Mrs. Elfand was already walking toward Mac. She stopped him in the middle of a windup. "What's the matter, Mrs. Elfand?" he asked. "Is there something wrong?"

I turned and leaned my shoulder into the fence. I didn't want to see what was happening. But I couldn't avoid hearing.

"Nothing's wrong," Mrs. Elfand said. "I just want you to let Henry and Benny play with you. You're only practicing."

"Oh, there's plenty of room closer to the building," Mac replied. "They can shag balls there if they want. We're going to start a game now."

"No, let them play with you," Mrs. Elfand said firmly. "We should develop a class team. Then we could challenge Miss O'Connor's class to a game in the park one afternoon."

"We play Miss O'Connor's class all the time," Mac said.

"I mean the *whole* class," Mrs. Elfand responded. "Our whole class. Don't forget, that ball and bat belong to the school! Come on, boys," she called. "Benny, Henry, come on. You can play now. Here, Benny, you stand behind Lancelot." (That was Double Dip.) "When he's done, you can hit a few. Henry, you go out there and stand in left field. Over there, on the other side of the walk."

Henry ran toward the cement walk. I shuffled slowly over to a position behind Double Dip. I tried

59

to make myself invisible, but it was hard. I was so big.

Mrs. Elfand moved away. At first I thought she was going back to stand on the front steps of the building. Then I could have sort of faded back to the security of the fence. But Mrs. Elfand took her job as playground monitor seriously. She just walked a few yards behind Fred LaPorta, the catcher, and turned to watch.

With a shrug that seemed to say, "Let's get this over with," Mac called out to Double Dip, "Give the bat to Benny. You pitch," he told Carlo, tossing the ball to him and moving back to a position between first and second base.

I picked up the bat. I put it over my shoulder and swung it a few times, just to get the feel of it. It was not a bat I'd used before, but it felt O.K. "Hurry up, Benny," Carlo called. "We ain't got all day."

I swung the bat once more. I knew what I was doing, and no one, not even Mac's pal, was going to rush me. Then I straightened my shoulders and nodded to Carlo. He threw the ball. It was high. I just stood there and let it go by.

"What's the matter, Benny?" Carlo called sarcastically. "You waitin' for a good one? All right, I'll give you a good one." He rubbed the ball between his sweaty palms. If Mrs. Elfand hadn't been watching, he'd have spit on it. Then threw it. It whizzed by. I swung and missed.

"One more and you're out," Carlo shouted.

"The first one was a ball," Mrs. Elfand called. "It didn't count. Anyway, you're just practicing. You're just hitting a few."

"My God," Fred muttered. "I never thought *she* knew anything about baseball."

Carlo wound up and pitched the ball again. This time my swing connected with a satisfying crack, and the ball whizzed straight and fast over the cement walk and past Henry, landing at last on the far side of the building in the seventh- and eighth-grade yard, out by the garbage pails. They all watched it go, and the only two people whose mouths hadn't dropped open in amazement were me and Henry.

Henry ran for the ball. "Lucky hit," Carlo said. "We gonna play a game now, Mac?"

"No," said Mac. "Hit a few more," he called out to me. "Hey, Henry, toss it here." Henry threw the ball to Mac, and it landed neatly in his glove. Mac always wore his own glove. He didn't share with the outfielders.

Mac must have pitched thirty balls while the others stood around and watched, or ran for the balls when they came in their direction. Mac pitched hard, but I hit the ball eighteen times. Henry kept count. Twice the ball went foul and four times someone caught it. The other dozen were good clean hits. Two sailed over the fence and into the street and Mac had to wait while Henry or Carlo went after it. After I had hit the ball about the fifteenth time, Mrs. Elfand went away.

When the bell rang signaling the end of recess, I turned to walk toward the building, still clutching the bat. We didn't have to line up to enter the building after recess. But I stopped and turned around when I heard Mac calling me. "Wait up," he said. He caught up to me in a second. "Here, Fred, you take these things in." He grabbed the bat out of my hand and shoved it at Fred, along with the ball. Fred walked off slowly, glancing behind him every once in a while, but Mac did not follow.

"Hey, Ben," Mac said to me, "where you been hiding yourself?"

"What do you mean?"

"When did you get to be a ballplayer? Nobody ever told me nothing about it."

"I been practicing," I said. "Me and Henry. But I don't run that good. I don't even know if I catch too good. I don't get much practice at that with Henry."

"I'm not worried about the other things," Mac said. "I need a hitter, that's what I need. And that's what you are. A slugger."

Henry came running up to us, out of breath. "Hey, you guys, the bell's rung. You better get in the building."

62

"Oh, get lost, will ya?" Mac said. "Mrs. Elfand will wait a second. It won't kill her."

But I started walking with Henry. "I'm in enough trouble with Mrs. Elfand as it is," I explained. "I don't need to be late."

"But I want to talk to you," Mac said.

"You can talk while you walk, can't you?" Henry asked.

"What I got to say ain't none of your beeswax," Mac answered. He didn't say it mean; he just said it.

"Look," I said, "Henry's my buddy. Everyone knows that."

"O.K., O.K.," Mac said. "But Henry can't play with us this afternoon. He can come and watch if he wants, but he can't play. He ain't good enough, and the rest of the guys on our team wouldn't like it."

"I don't have to play," Henry inserted quickly. "I don't even want to play. But Benny, he sure wants to play."

"Yeah, I want to play," I said. Boy, did I ever. I could feel how badly I wanted it in my hands and the muscles of my arms. "But I can't play," I had to say. "Not this afternoon. I gotta watch the store while my dad makes deliveries."

"Can't you come just for a little while?" Mac urged. "We all got to leave at five or five-thirty anyway."

63

By this time we had reached our classroom. Everyone else was already seated, their songbooks out on their desks. We always had music first thing after recess.

"I can't come," I whispered hurriedly. "My dad delivers between three-thirty and five."

"Just once?" Mac insisted. "Just this once. We gotta beat those guys from Hamilton." I pretended not to hear him as I ran for my seat in the back of the room. I leaned down and peered inside my desk for a long moment, as if searching for my songbook. Saying no to Mac was the toughest thing I'd ever done. To have other friends besides Henry—above all to have Mac for a friend—it was a thing so marvelous I could barely imagine it. I began to feel very sorry for myself. They, whoever they were, wouldn't let such a good thing happen to me. They wouldn't let it happen to Benny Rifkind. *He* couldn't be part of Mac's gang. He had to go home and help his father in the store.

"Are you planning to join us this afternoon?" Mrs. Elfand said sharply. "Benny, do you hear me? Sit up." There wasn't much time for self-pity in Mrs. Elfand's class. I pulled my songbook out hastily and opened it. "Page eighty-two," Mrs. Elfand said. She blew a note on her pitch pipe. "We'll try a new one today, 'Stout-Hearted Men,' if Benny is ready."

I felt my face go hot with embarrassment, but once we started singing, I forgot all of that. It was a good song:

"Give me some men who are stout-hearted men,
Who will fight for the right they adore. . . ."

I had had to say no to Mac, but at least he had
asked me. That was an important thing.

seven

Unfortunately, after school I began to think maybe it would have been better if I hadn't been asked. As I walked down the steps, Mac was at my side again. He had Carlo with him. Carlo walked on my other side. They were like a pair of gangsters in an Edward G. Robinson movie. "Listen," Mac said, "if you told your father, if you explained to him how important this is. . ."

"My father doesn't think baseball is important," I told him.

"If you came anyway, what would he do?" Carlo asked. "Would he beat you up?"

"Beat me up? My father?"

"I didn't think so," Carlo said. "I know your father. So what're you afraid of? Come on."

"I can't," I said. "I just can't." Carlo didn't understand that there were worse hurts than the ones you got when people hit you.

"You don't want to very much, do you?" Mac said angrily. "Henry was wrong. You don't want to. Well, I don't ask twice. Don't you forget that. Come on, Carlo. Let's go. We don't want to be late."

Mac and Carlo sprinted off in the direction of the park. Henry went with them. He said he was going to watch the game whether I was playing in it or not.

I walked slowly down Bond Street in the opposite direction, my hands in my pockets. I tried to whistle. I tried "Stout-Hearted Men" but I couldn't remember the tune. "Gee-sus," I said, out loud. "Gee-sus." Nothing went right for me. Not ever.

When I got to the store, I saw Mr. Nussbaum coming out carrying a paper bag. I knew it held no more than a pint of milk, a small loaf of bread, and maybe a half-dozen eggs or a small can of salmon. Mr. Nussbaum was retired and did all the shopping for his wife and himself. Since he didn't have anything else to do, he made sure he shopped every day, some days twice.

"Hello, Andson," Mr. Nussbaum said. That was his idea of a joke. He called me "Andson" whenever he saw me. He had called Sheldon "Andson" too when Sheldon had worked in the store. This was because the peeling gilt letters on the store window read, *M.H. Rifkind and Son, Grocers, est. 1920.* Mr. Nussbaum knew as well as anyone else that my father was not M.H. Rifkind. M.H. Rifkind was my grandfather, and he'd died when I was a baby. My own father, Jacob Rifkind, was the real "Andson." I wondered why Pop had never changed that sign.

"Hello, Mr. Nussbaum," I said.

"I think your father's waiting for you," Mr. Nussbaum said. "He has his coat on. Whenever he has his coat on, he gets that—"

Mr. Nussbaum certainly didn't have to tell me my father was waiting for me. "I know, I know," I interrupted him. It was boring in the store, but it was more boring standing on the sidewalk listening to Mr. Nussbaum, who could easily go on for half an hour. "I gotta go." I pushed open the door and walked in the store. Instantly my nostrils were full of the grocery store smell, a mixture of pickles and oiled floors and something stale. Other people liked that smell, but I couldn't stand it.

The room was dim and it was a moment before my eyes became accustomed enough to the light to see my father. He was behind the rear counter, his back to me, talking on the telephone, which was mounted on the wall.

"Call about five-thirty, Goldie," I heard him say. "She'll certainly be up then. . . . No, you won't

68

interrupt our dinner. We don't eat until seven, after I close the store. . . . Yes, well, keep a stiff upper lip, Goldie. We'll be over Sunday. Sheldon and Benny will take him for a walk or play catch with him or something. . . . O.K. . . . I have to make deliveries now. We'll see you Sunday. Good-bye."

I stepped behind the counter as Pop hung up the phone. I took a big white apron from the bottom shelf and tied in on. Last year I had to hike it up around my waist so it wouldn't drag on the floor. No more. "Is Ma still taking her nap?" I asked.

"Yes," Pop replied. "That's why she didn't pick up the phone upstairs, and I got involved in a long conversation with your Aunt Goldie. It was so long, even Mr. Nussbaum got discouraged and left. But I don't blame Goldie for wanting to talk. She's got her hands full, God knows."

"What's the matter?" I couldn't imagine any situation Goldie couldn't deal with.

"Remember the German refugee boy you met at her house a few months ago? Arnulf Schneider?"

"How could I forget? What a snot!"

"Well, it seems he couldn't get along with those people he'd come here with where they'd gone to live in Philadelphia, and now he's with Goldie and Moe. He's some kind of cousin to Moe, you know. He's not getting along too well with them either. Can you imagine anyone not getting along with your Aunt Goldie?"

I shook my head.

"And if he can't get along with Goldie, can you imagine what's going on with Moe and the girls?"

I understood what my father meant. Essie was almost as easy-going as her mother, but Sylvia and Moe were another story.

"Boy, oh boy," I said. "Now we can't even enjoy talking to Aunt Goldie when we go there on a Sunday. Another lousy thing."

"What do you mean, *another* lousy thing?" Pop asked.

"Nothing went right today," I told him. Then I remembered all those times I had hit the ball, and I realized that wasn't quite true. "Almost nothing," I corrected myself.

"Like what?"

"It's not important."

"Tell me."

I decided not to mention the possibility of my staying back. I picked another thing to tell him about, even thought I knew it would sound silly to him. "Mac wanted me to play ball with him this afternoon and I couldn't because I had to come to work."

"Mac? Who's Mac?"

"This kid. He's new this year. James MacDonald. Everyone calls him Mac."

"So what's so special, playing ball with him? You can play with Henry when I get back."

I reached under the counter for my Hebrew book. Now that I had to stay in the store, I couldn't

70

go to Hebrew school to study for my bar mitzvah, and I was trying to keep up on my own. "That's what I said," I explained. "It's not important."

"It certainly doesn't sound important enough to get upset over, does it?" Pop said. "It didn't really ruin the whole day. You're exaggerating."

All right, I thought, I'd try. It was hopeless, but I'd try anyway. "You see, Pop, it's like this. Everyone likes Mac. He's sort of . . . well . . . he's sort of the leader I guess you could say. . . ."

"You'll tell me when I get back, Benny. I've got to get this stuff to the ladies so they can make dinner."

Well, I had known it wouldn't be any use. There was no way to make my father understand. He would have liked to understand. He just couldn't. He just didn't have the time. Or maybe not the concentration, with all he had to worry about. As for baseball, to my father that was just a game. It had nothing to do with real life. I knew I wouldn't bring the subject up again. All I said was, "O.K., Pop. See you later."

He had already loaded most of the orders, but we carried out the last few cardboard boxes filled with groceries and put them into the back of the 1931 Chevy pickup truck. "Don't do anything I wouldn't do," Pop called to me as he climbed into the cab. "Don't break any eggs." He smiled, but I didn't feel like smiling back. I just waved as he pulled away from the curb.

71

eight

Before supper, my father always listened to Lowell Thomas on station WJZ. He tried to get the rest of us to listen too, but we didn't really want to very much. Lowell Thomas kept talking about the gathering war clouds in Europe and Ma found the idea of another war too depressing to even think about. Evvie was always busy in the kitchen getting dinner. She wanted it all eaten and cleaned up by eight o'clock so she could go for a walk with Morty Katz. Sheldon said he couldn't spare the time, but that was because anything which didn't directly concern Sheldon didn't really interest Sheldon. I guess, though, the same was true for me. I found Lowell Thomas very boring when I listened to him, which wasn't often. In nice weather I was out on the street or in the alley with Henry until Evvie or my mother leaned out of the window and called me up for supper.

But on this night Henry had not come around to the store at five or five-thirty as he usually did. I figured maybe the game in the park had run late, or maybe he had even done something with one of the other guys afterward. So I was in the living room, trying to do my arithmetic homework and half-listening to Lowell Thomas. Even Lowell Thomas could distract me from arithmetic, especially since he was talking about the World's Fair.

"Attendance at the New York World's Fair," Lowell Thomas said, "was today again far below expectations of fair officials. Fair president Grover Whalen's prediction of a crowd of one million yesterday for opening day scared off many potential visitors, and today so far, fewer than one hundred thousand people have gone through the turnstiles, according to the National Cash Register Company's seven-story cash register which keeps a running record of fair attendance. But the fair's festive atmosphere was heightened today by the presence of the King and Queen of Norway, the first in a long parade of royal visitors. The king officially opened the Norwegian pavilion. . . ."

I remembered the description I had read in Sunday's paper about the World of Tomorrow. "You know, Pop," I said, "we ought to go to the fair. If the crowds aren't so big as they expected, I bet we could get there easy. We ought to go soon, before all those kings and queens and everybody mob the place up."

"Maybe you're right," Pop responded thoughtfully.

"I'd sure like to see that World of Tomorrow," I added.

"Me too," he said. "I'd really like to see it all."

"Anybody would," I told him. "Even Sheldon."

"Well then, let's go!" Pop said suddenly. "What are we waiting for? Next Sunday we have to go to Goldie, but let's go the Sunday after that."

"All of us?" I couldn't believe he'd accepted the idea so quickly. He must have been as excited about the fair as I was.

"All of us," he said. "I'm sure Sheldon'll take the day off for the fair. Evvie can even bring Morty Katz if she wants to."

"Can we afford it?" I found myself listing all the things that might stand in our way. I didn't want him changing his mind later. That would have been too disappointing for me to bear.

"It won't be that expensive," he replied. "We can bring our lunch. Of course, it all depends on how your mother feels," he added hastily. "We're going to the doctor Thursday. We'll ask him. I know a

74

change of scene, a little distraction, will do her a world of good. We all need a little reward. We've all been working very hard."

I jumped up out of my seat. "I'm going to tell Evvie," I said. If other people knew about it, it had more chance of actually happening.

Pop nodded. "O.K., but don't forget it all depends on how your mother feels." I wasn't too worried about my mother. She was always ailing, even before the operation, but I had noticed that whenever there was some place good to go, like a wedding or Bradley Beach, she got better fast.

I ran through the dining room and into the kitchen like a tornado. The fair. The World's Fair. I was going to get to go. Something good was going to happen to me at last. I was going to fly past the villages and cities of the World of Tomorrow, free as a bird. Really, it hadn't been such a bad day after all. Even if I might have to stay back in the sixth grade another year because I couldn't do arithmetic, and even if I did have to sit around in that boring, dark, smelly store for two hours every afternoon, I could whistle, sing, hit balls, and wait for the Sunday after next. Even if Mac was mad at me. Even if Mac never spoke to me again.

nine

But Mac did speak to me the very next day, during recess. I tried to avoid him. When the lunch bell rang, I went up to Mrs. Elfand and asked her if there was anything I could do for her during the break. She looked at me a little oddly. No wonder. I had never made such an offer before. But she replied pleasantly enough, "Thank you very much, Benny. It's nice of you to offer, but really, there's nothing. I'm going to the teachers' room to eat. I can't let you stay in here alone while I'm gone. It's against the rules. You know that."

"Yeah . . . well . . ." I tried to think of something else to say, but I couldn't, so I just stood there.

"Thanks again," she repeated. When I didn't move, her usual sharpness returned. "Get out of here now," she ordered. "I don't want to miss my lunch. Go ahead. Go outside.

I went. I thought maybe I'd be lucky and by this time Henry might have given up on me and gone over by himself to watch Mac's gang play. On our way to school, he'd told me that he was going to go to all the games Mac's gang played. He was too old to be their mascot, but he could be a sort of professional rooter. Though others came to see the games, Mac had let Henry sit with the guys when the team was at bat. They didn't let anyone else do that.

But when I walked out of the building, there was old faithful Henry waiting for me. "I don't want to watch the guys play," I said immediately. "You go yourself. I'll just sit right here on the steps. I don't feel too good."

"Mac told me to wait for you," Henry said. "He said to make sure you came over to practice."

"But he was so mad at me yesterday afternoon," I said in wonder.

"So he got mad," Henry replied with a shrug of his shoulders. "People get mad all the time and say things they don't mean. Of course, Mac usually

77

means what he says, but he needs you, Benny. He really needs you."

I went over then and practiced with Mac and the other guys. This time I just took my regular turn at bat, and I controlled myself so I wouldn't hit the ball over the fence. When we started to play a game, my side won three to nothing. We only had time for two innings.

Afterward, Mac walked over to me. Before he could open his mouth, I opened mine. "I can't play today after school either. I gotta work. I gotta work every day."

"I understand, I understand," Mac said. "I mean, I really do. Besides, we don't have a game this afternoon anyway. Only twice a week, or three times at most."

"How did you do yesterday?" I knew they'd won. Henry had told me. But I pretended I didn't know in order to have something to say.

"We won," Mac replied. "Easily. Seven to two. I knew we would."

"Then what. . ?" I began involuntarily. What did you need me for, is what I meant to say, but realizing that might sound like a criticism of Mac, I shut up.

Mac knew what I meant. "I wanted to make sure you were as good as you seemed," he said. "It really wasn't an important game. The important game is one week from today, next Tuesday, when we play the guys who hang out at the YMCA. They beat us last week. I don't want that to happen again. Now, you make sure you come to that one. You tell your father it's the only time. He's gotta let you out that once."

"Why can't the game be Saturday sometime?" I suggested. "I don't have to be in the store all day Saturday. Sometimes I go to the movies. We could play instead." I had a lot of nerve, telling Mac when to play, but Mac seemed to want me so badly. Still, I should have known better.

"That's pretty dumb," Mac said. "Where'm I gonna find all those guys to tell them the game's changed? I don't even know the names of half of 'em. Last week after we lost we made up the game was gonna be on Tuesday, and that's when it's gonna be. I want to spring a little surprise on 'em." Mac shook his head and said in a mild voice, "I hate those guys. They think they're something big. So you'll talk to your dad, huh? From what Carlo says, he's a nice guy."

"O.K.," I said. "I'll try. I can't promise anything, but I'll try." I couldn't just say no to Mac. Not flat out. Anyway, Tuesday was a whole week away. A lot could happen in a week. If I didn't say no right off, at least I'd have a whole week of playing ball with the guys during recess and a whole week of walking into the school afterward with Mac.

ten

Sunday we all went to visit Goldie and Moe. Sheldon had tried to get out of it again. But again Pop had made him go. "Goldie needs you boys today," he said. "Maybe you can do something with the refugee. Maybe you can talk to him or something, try to straighten him out a little. Sometimes kids will listen to other kids when they won't listen to grown-ups."

"The whole United States Army couldn't straighten that kid out," I said.

"Try to have a little compassion, Benny," Pop went on. "The boy is just about your age, and he's separated from his parents. He must be worried about them all the time. It's enough to make a grown-up act strange, let alone a young kid."

But after we had had dinner with him, even Pop had trouble finding compassion in his heart for Arnulf Schneider. When we arrived, Goldie said to Essie, "Go upstairs and tell Arnulf the Rifkinds are here. Tell him the boys would like to play with him."

"Play?" Sheldon asked, his eyebrows raised.

"You know what I mean, Sheldon," Goldie answered testily.

"Benny can play with him," Sheldon told her.

"Well, then," Goldie said, "you can talk to him."

Meanwhile, Essie hadn't moved. "Go ahead, Essie," her mother repeated. "Go get Arnulf."

"You want him, get him yourself," Essie said. "You know what he called me the last time I 'interrupted' him, as he puts it? An 'interfering American idiot!' What does he do up there in his room all the time? And for him we had to throw out that nice boarder from Scranton."

"Listen, Essie," her mother pointed out, "it's been a lot better around here since he started that scientific project of his."

Moe nodded his agreement. "At least he isn't with us *all* the time," he said.

"He's trying to blow us up. I know it," Essie insisted.

"Don't talk foolish," her mother scolded.

"Well," Sylvia chimed in, "I notice that you gave him money for all that copper tubing and electric wire he needed. When I want a new pair of shoes, you can't afford them."

I had never heard Goldie's family bicker before. I knew they did in private, like other families; sometimes I heard about it from Goldie or one of the girls. But I had never seen them fall apart in public this way. "Well," I said, "I'll go up and get him."

"Oh, that's fine." Goldie seemed relieved. "You know the room—the first door on the right at the top of the stairs."

"Make sure you knock," Essie warned.

I knocked. A voice called out from inside the room, "What is it? Why are you bothering me now? I am very busy." The pronunciation was careful and precise, but almost unaccented, a big improvement since February.

"It's me, Benny Rifkind," I said. "Do you remember me from the last time you were here?"

"No," answered the voice, "I don't."

"You want to come out and play catch or something?" I wasn't finding it easy to keep up my end of the conversation through a closed door.

"No," the voice replied. "I don't. Throwing a ball around is a waste of time."

That was something my mother or father would say, not a kid. I was seriously considering leaving when suddenly the door opened. There stood Arnulf in short pants, a shirt, tie, and sweater. He wore high socks and heavy walking shoes. He was only about half my size. He looked me up and down with his small, darting brown eyes, set deep within dark hollows. "I remember you now. You are Mrs. Glaser's nephew." I had to think a minute before I realized that Mrs. Glaser was Goldie. No one ever referred to her as anything but Goldie, except her own children when they called her "Ma."

"That's right," I said.

"I don't play American games," Arnulf said. "They have no point."

I bit my tongue so I wouldn't say what I wanted to say. What I did say was, "Well, maybe you'd like to come down and talk to my brother. He's very smart. You could tell him about your experiment. He's going to Cooper Union to be an engineer."

"I have no interest in engineering," Arnulf replied. "I am concerned only with pure science. My father is a professor of chemistry at the University of Heidelberg. When was Cooper Union founded? Heidelberg was founded in 1386. I have never heard of Cooper Union."

"Well, I have never heard of the University of Heidelberg," I retorted.

"I wouldn't expect that you had," Arnulf replied calmly. "Americans don't know much."

"Why don't you go back to Germany then?" I couldn't help but ask.

"Oh, I will," Arnulf responded confidently. "I will very soon. My parents will send for me as soon as this Hitler business blows over."

I heard footsteps coming up the stairs. I turned and there was Sylvia. "Essie, Sheldon, Evvie, and I are going for a walk," she said. "We're going over to visit the Levy kids. You two don't want to come, do you? You'd be bored. They're all too old for you." It was perfectly obvious that she didn't want us to come, at least not Arnulf, and had issued the invitation only because her mother had insisted.

"You are correct, Sylvia," Arnulf said. "I don't want to come. The Levys are very shallow people. Benny can go if he wishes. Or he can stay with me. I can show him my experiment." He looked directly at me. "Would you please stay, Benny?" There was the merest touch of softness in his voice.

I was taken aback. I couldn't refuse a direct request like that. He seemed to really want me to stay. It occurred to me that he was horribly lonesome.

"I'll stay," I said. "I won't be missing anything at the Levys'."

"Why, that's wonderful," Sylvia cried with such delight you'd think someone had just handed her a hundred dollar bill. "Benny will love looking at your experiment, won't you, Benny? You should

84

feel honored. Arnulf hasn't shown it to anyone yet."

I followed Arnulf into the bedroom and looked around. Next to the narrow bed, a nightstand was piled with books. The open space between the dresser and bed was full of tubing, wire, glass bottles, and even an electric hot plate. I couldn't make anything out of all that junk but I was impressed. Arnulf must be smarter even than Sheldon.

The top of the dresser was empty except for three pictures, two women and a man. One of the women was a really sensational looking blonde. I picked my way through the equipment on the floor and took the picture in my hands. "This is sure a pretty lady," I said. "Is she your mother?"

"Put that picture down," Arnulf said angrily. "I said you could look. I didn't say you could touch anything."

"O.K., O.K.," I said, hastily returning the photograph to its resting place on the bureau. "I'm sorry. I didn't mean anything by it."

"No, of course not," Arnulf responded. "No American ever *means* to be rude. You just *are*, that's all."

"And Germans aren't, not ever, is that it?" I asked sarcastically.

"Europeans in general are more polite," Arnulf said. "Even Americans admit that."

I decided to show him. I'd be polite. "May I please sit down?" I asked.

"Certainly," Arnulf replied, bowing his head graciously. He gestured toward the bed. "You may sit down there while I explain my experiment." He crossed to the front of the dresser and then turned to face me as if he were his father, the professor of chemistry at the University of Heidelberg, about to deliver a lecture. "But first," he said generously, "since you were kind enough to express an interest, I will explain the pictures. The lady you admired is not my mother. She is my stepmother. My own mother died when I was five. She is the lady in the other picture. She is just as pretty, perhaps not quite as . . ." He hesitated a moment, searching for the right word. "Not quite as chic," he finished. "My stepmother, however, loves me very much. She is not like the stepmother in 'Hansel and Gretel.' She cried the whole night before I left. She loves me very much, and so does my father."

"Well, naturally," I said.

"No, not naturally," Arnulf insisted. "Don't you know there are lots of mothers and fathers who don't love their children?"

"Well, maybe. No one I know."

Arnulf knelt down among his equipment. "You are so innocent, so naive," he said, shaking his head. "Like all Americans. How old are you, Benny?"

"I'll be thirteen in January." We had discussed our ages the last time I'd met him, but he didn't remember.

"I won't be thirteen until next March," he said, "but I am older than you are. So much older." For once, there was no superiority in his voice, only a kind of terrible sadness.

"How come you know English so well?" I asked, changing the subject. "You spoke it pretty good even when you were here in February, and you'd only just come then."

Arnulf's hands were busy connecting bottles and tubes, but he didn't seem to find that any obstacle to continuing the conversation. "German schools are much better than American schools," he said, back in stride. "I began studying English when I was seven. My stepmother spoke English to me a lot. Her mother was an Englishwoman."

"Why did you leave those people in Philadelphia?" I asked. "The ones you came over with."

"It was my parents' idea that I come with them," Arnulf replied acidly. "I didn't want to come with them. I knew from the beginning they were stupid people. I didn't want to come at all. But Father made me come. He was afraid for me, because I'm Jewish."

That was funny. "I'm Jewish," not "We're Jewish."

"Why didn't your parents come too?" I asked.

"Oh, they're not Jewish. They're pure Aryan," Arnulf said. He said it proudly, as if it were something to boast of. "I'm only half Jewish, really, on account of my mother."

"The one who's dead."

"Yes. The one who's dead." Suddenly, with an angry gesture, he pulled the tube out of the bottle he was holding. "This isn't going to work," he said. "It isn't ready."

"Well, what is it?" I asked. "What's it going to be?"

"You wouldn't understand," Arnulf said. "You haven't had enough education. You don't really want to know anyway. You're just being nice. That's the way Americans are. They aren't really interested in you. They just have to be nice."

"I'm really interested," I insisted. "I want to know. I really do." I really didn't. It wasn't his experiment I was interested in. It was him. He was crazy, but then so's everyone else—at least, everyone else who's even a little bit interesting.

"Well, all right then," Arnulf said. His voice implied that what was to follow was some kind of test. "I'll try to explain it to you. What I'm doing is studying this new sulfa compound I bought in the pharmacy." He held up a little glass jar filled with a yellow powder. "In order to see what it's really made out of, I have to crystallize it. The question was, how? There are several methods of crystallization, you know." He paused, staring at the powder in the jar.

"Oh," I said. "I didn't know."

"Here. I'll tell you about them. I had to read about the different methods in order to select the one I wanted to use." He picked up a book from the night table and began reading from it out loud. "Crystallization may be accomplished either from the fused state or from solution, the latter being by far the best and most common method. When an impure substance is cooled below its melting point, it may crystallize. However, if cooling is continued until the entire material is solid, obviously no purification has taken place; the substance has merely changed in state from a liquid to a solid. If the substance is only partly frozen, the crystals formed probably will be pure but will be wet with liquid containing the impurity. By decanting the liquid . . ."

Arnulf was obviously fascinated by what he was reading because he read it with considerable excitement in his voice. However, I found it very hard to follow, and after a while I just couldn't concentrate on it anymore. I didn't want to insult Arnulf by saying anything or moving from my position on the bed, but my eyes wandered around the room. From where I was sitting, I really couldn't see anything out of the window except the top of a tree. There were no birds or squirrels in it that I could notice. There were no pictures on the walls, and the wallpaper was nothing but the same little pink flower repeated over and over again on a faded pale blue background. It was very hot in that little room, terribly hot for so early in May.

A newspaper lay beside me on the red and white

chenille bedspread, open and folded to reveal half a page. It was *The New York Times.* My eye fell upon it and I began to read. *"The Weather Over the Nation.* Fair and continued warm weather is forecast for today. Tomorrow will be cooler and increasingly cloudy, with showers in the afternoon or at night. . . . Pressure is high off the South Atlantic Coast and thence eastward beyond Bermuda. It is high also off the New England coast, over Maine and the Maritime Provinces." Cripes, that was dull. Who cared about the weather in the Maritime Provinces, wherever they were.

Next I glanced at *Shipping and Mails.* "SAIL TUESDAY (MAY 9). *Transatlantic. Black Condor.* (Black Diamond) Rotterdam, May 22 and Antwerp, May 26 (mails close 8:00 A.M.). Pier K, Weehawken. Parcel Post only for Belgium, Belgian Congo, Luxembourg and Netherlands. LATER SAILINGS. Wednesday, May 10. *Transatlantic. New York* (Hamburg American) . . . Hamburg. *President Harding* (United States) . . . Hamburg. *Queen Mary* (Cunard White Star) . . . Southampton." There was more, lots more, but it wasn't any more interesting than the weather. Why would anyone want to read this page of *The New York Times* when the very same paper had a whole section devoted to sports, even if it was without a single comic strip?

I had almost forgotten about Arnulf. I turned a

90

page to look for the sports section, oblivious of his voice still droning on: "The first step, selection of a suitable solvent, is sometimes difficult. If the substance is known, a solvent for crystallization has usually been reported in the literature . . ."

The paper rattled and Arnulf looked up. "You're not listening," he said with exasperation. "I knew it. I knew you weren't really interested."

"I'm certainly not interested in that book," I said. "I think I'd be interested in what *you* have to say."

"You can't understand the experiment unless you have the proper background," Arnulf said, slamming the volume shut.

"Hey, don't be mad at me," I said. "Maybe if you showed that book to Sheldon, he could explain it to me. He understands stuff like that."

"You just want to see bubbles and explosions. That's all chemistry means to you," Arnulf interrupted derisively.

"Chemistry doesn't mean anything to me," I admitted. "Nothing at all. But I'd like to find out about it. I'd like you to tell me. Only you have to explain it to me in words that I can understand. You have to show me something."

"Well." He seemed a little mollified. "There's nothing I can show you. Not yet. It isn't ready yet."

"When it's ready," I said, "call me up." I meant it. "I'll come to see it. I'll take a streetcar and come by myself. You don't have to wait for a Sunday.

And I think I'll ask my buddy Henry if he's read anything about chemistry in one of his magazines. Then maybe I'll understand more next time."

"All right," Arnulf said. "I'll call you when I'm ready. Maybe I'll be able to find a really simple chemistry book for you if I stop in the children's room at the library tomorrow."

I wanted to tell him the book didn't have to be all that simple, but I didn't. He meant to be kind, he really did. It was just hard for him, that's all. He was in a terrible situation. I could understand that. So instead I said, "Thanks, Arnulf. I appreciate that. I guess you're smarter even than Henry. Maybe you're as smart as Sheldon."

"Well, I thank you too," Arnulf said stiffly. "You may not know much, but perhaps you're really nice, not just nice on the top, like most Americans."

"I hope so," I said. I couldn't think of anything else to say on that subject, but I didn't have to. We were interrupted by a knock on the bedroom door.

"What do you want?" Arnulf called. "We're busy."

Essie's voice answered. "Come on downstairs. It's time for dinner."

"I don't want any dinner," Arnulf said.

"You have to eat," Essie replied. "A person has to eat."

"I don't want any dinner," Arnulf repeated in a louder, firmer tone.

"Well, I do," I said. "I'll see you later, Arnulf."
I got up from the bed, picked my way across the
floor, and opened the door.

"Wasn't it delightful?" Essie whispered as we
walked down the stairs. "Wasn't it just the most
delightful hour of your entire life?"

"Oh yeah," I agreed, automatically echoing her
sarcasm. "I loved every second of it." But then I
added, "You know, there's something wrong with
him."

"You're telling me!" Essie exclaimed.

"No . . . no . . . that's not what I mean. Something's bothering him. That's why he's the way he
is."

"I know it isn't easy to go through what he's gone
through," Essie admitted, "but knowing that doesn't
make it any easier to live with him. Ma says, 'Make
allowances.' A person can't go around making allowances forever. I've got to live too." By this time we
had reached the dining room, where steaming plat-
ters of pot roast and potato pancakes were already
laid out on the table. "He's not coming," Essie
announced. "He doesn't want any dinner."

Goldie's face fell. "But we have such a good
dinner. He's so thin. What's he trying to do?"

"Starve himself to death, like Mahatma Gandhi,"
Sylvia said.

"Let's eat before he changes his mind," Essie
said. "We'll enjoy our dinner more without him."

Goldie was too honest a person to argue with that

93

statement. But she had barely finished heaping each of our plates with food when he appeared and slipped into the empty chair.

"Oh, Arnulf, I'm glad you decided to come down," Goldie said, forcing a smile into her voice. "We have a very good dinner."

"The best," Moe added. "Pot roast."

"I don't like pot roast," Arnulf said.

"Not like pot roast!" Moe exclaimed. "I never heard of anyone not liking pot roast."

"Now you have," Arnulf announced.

"Don't get fresh with me, young man," Moe warned. "I don't put up with it from my own children; I won't put up with it from you."

"American children are all fresh," Arnulf said. "Fresh or sneaky. Essie and Sylvia do anything they want, and you don't say anything to them. They just act sweet in front of you, but do you really know what they're doing? I never do anything wrong. I just tell the truth, that's all."

"What are you talking about, Arnulf Schneider?" Essie said. "How dare you talk like that? I don't do anything behind my parents' back."

Arnulf smiled at her. "Not even when you—how do you say it?—*neck* with the boys on the front porch? Alvin one night and Billy another night and Si the night after that. My goodness, you're busy!"

Essie turned white. "A spy!" she screamed. "You're a spy! What do you do at night, lean out of your bedroom window and watch me instead of sleeping?"

"You don't deny it, do you?" Arnulf said. "It's true, isn't it?"

"Do you know what you really are?" Essie said. Her voice was calmer now. "You're a Nazi. That's what all Germans are. Spies and snakes. And that's what you are." She got up from the table and turned to her father. "As long as he sits at this table, I won't."

"He didn't mean it," Goldie said. "He's just talking the way a brother would talk. You'd know that if you'd ever had one, like I did."

"He's not my brother, thank God. And I wouldn't take it from him if he was."

"I did mean it," Arnulf said to Goldie. "I never say what I don't mean."

"Essie, I'll speak to you later," Moe interrupted. "Arnulf, you can go back to your room. Cousin Goldie will bring you a sandwich later." Arnulf left quickly, as if glad to escape the chaos he had created. It was the oddest thing I had ever seen. He deliberately baited all of them. He had been almost nice to me, alone in his room. If he had been just that nice to Goldie and no nicer, she would have loved him. But with them, this wonderful family, this almost perfect family, he was at his worst, and they didn't even know he could be any better.

We didn't see Essie again for the rest of the afternoon. We didn't stay much longer anyway. Conversation kind of dragged during the remainder of the meal. Certainly Goldie didn't tell us any of her usual jokes and stories. Moe was even quieter than usual, and with Essie gone, Sylvia seemed to have nothing to say. Ma made a few remarks about her visit to the doctor the previous Thursday. Pop brought up the danger in Prime Minister Chamberlain's hemming and hawing over the free city of Danzig. Evvie mentioned that she hoped the weather would be as fine next Sunday as this Sunday, for our trip to the World's Fair. That caused a small flurry of conversation.

"The lines at the General Motors exhibit are very long," Sylvia said. "My friend Betty Levy told me. She was there Wednesday."

"I bet Arnulf would like the Allied Chemical exhibit," I said, without thinking. The mere mention of Arnulf's name brought about perfect silence at the table. I stared down at my plate, busily shoving food in my mouth.

"Boy, Benny, you always do manage to say the wrong thing," Sheldon told me. He had to make a comment, of course. At least it was better than that unnatural quiet.

Evvie and Ma helped Goldie and Sylvia clean up in record time. Then we left. We were all really glad to get out of there.

eleven

On Monday, Mac didn't say one single word about the big game Tuesday afternoon. He didn't bug me the way he had every day the previous week. I was happy I didn't have to answer a direct question as to whether or not I'd be at the game. I knew he more or less simply expected me to show up. I should never have raised his hopes with my "I'll try" and "I'll ask." I should have told Mac in so many words that I wouldn't be there. But I just couldn't bring my mouth to utter those words. One more recess—Tuesday's. At least I could have that.

Arnulf had said I was really nice. I certainly wasn't being really nice to Mac. It isn't really nice to mislead a person who's supposed to be your friend. Well, part of the problem was Mac didn't really want my friendship. All he wanted was my good right arm.

Early Monday evening when my father came back to the store from making his deliveries, I did not dash out the door the first second I could, even though at the moment there were no customers. This was unusual, because between five o'clock and six-thirty was usually a busy time.

"Is there something else I can do for you, Pop?" I asked. "I dusted all the shelves and I picked the rotten apples out of the barrel and I put away all those cans of corn and peas that were delivered this morning. There didn't seem to be any room for the Ivory Snow, but if you want me to put some of the Rinso in the back room . . ."

"You must be after something," Pop laughed. "What is it, Benny? You don't have to go through all these machinations. Just tell me."

"I thought you'd be glad I shelved all those cans."

"I am. Thank you. Now, what is it?"

There was nothing to do but ask right out. I didn't think I had worked so hard all afternoon just to get on my father's good side, but maybe that was so. "Look, Pop," I said. "I want to play ball tomorrow afternoon. It's a very important game, with the

YMCA, and they want me on the team. They never did before."

"Well, I'm sorry, son," he said, "but you can't. You've got to be here, in the store. You know that."

"But it's just this once," I pleaded. "I kind of promised Mac, you know. Just this once Sheldon or Evvie could come down, couldn't they?"

"Sheldon has more important things to do than give you the chance to play baseball," Pop said. He was no longer amused. "You play enough ball."

"But this is different," I tried to explain. "This is an important game, and they just let me be on the team. Just last week. I don't see why Sheldon couldn't help me this once. Or Evvie."

"Evvie has work to do. And it wouldn't be this once. You know that. It would happen again and again and again. Times are hard, Benny. We manage, but only if we all work together. Only if we all cooperate."

I had heard all that so many times I could repeat it in my sleep. "You've got to learn what's important, Benny," Pop continued. "Making a living is important. It's the most important thing. You're old enough to understand that."

"Yes, Pop," I said. "I know. I know all of that. Listen, Pop. You're going to be proud of me one day. I know it."

"Am I?" he asked, with what sounded like genuine curiosity. Then he added quickly, "Of course

I'll be proud of you someday. You're a good boy, Benny. Don't think I don't know that, just because I get annoyed sometimes."

"So what would be so terrible," I begged, "if I played in the game tomorrow? Just tomorrow. Just this once."

Doc Woronoff came in on his way home from his drugstore. "Be right with you, Doc," my father called. Then he turned back to me. "Don't ask me again, Benny," he said firmly. "You'll be here tomorrow, and you'll be here on time, and you'll be here all afternoon. That's all there is to that."

There was nothing more to say. I walked out of the store. I didn't even answer Doc Woronoff when he said "Hello." What the devil was I going to say to Mac the next day? In the end, I decided to say nothing. I hadn't promised Mac, not really. I had just said I'd try. Well, I *had* tried. And I couldn't. And there was nothing I could do about it.

twelve

The next day, Tuesday, after recess practice, Mac and I walked back to the classroom together. Luckily, Carlo and Henry were with us so the conversation remained general. Mainly it was about the Giants-Cubs game the night before and how Carl Hubbell's relief pitching retired the Cubs on four pitches in the eighth inning but still couldn't save the game for the Giants.

As we separated inside the classroom, Mac whispered, "See you after school." I didn't answer. I didn't say yes. I didn't say no. I was a coward, that's all.

When three o'clock came, I ran out of the building like a bat out of hell. I was already on Main Street when I heard a voice calling, "Benny. Hey Benny!"

I turned around. Half a block behind me was Carlo. He was running, waving, and shouting all at once. "Hey, Benny, wait. Wait up."

I figured I'd better wait. I leaned up against the plate glass window in front of MacIntyre's Dry Goods and Notions, my hands in my pockets.

Carlo was huffing and puffing when he finally caught up to me. But he didn't wait to catch his breath before he started talking. "Hey, Benny," he said between gulps of air, "what's the big idea?"

"What d'ya mean, what's the big idea?"

"You know what I mean, Benny. Mac wants to know why you're going home. He wants to know why you're not going to the park for the game."

"He sent you after me to find out? I must be pretty important if he went to all that trouble." I was kidding, of course, but Carlo took me seriously.

"When we came out of school," he said, "Mac saw you turning right instead of left, and he said to me, 'Run after Benny. Find out why he ain't going to the park.' That's what he said. But are you ever tough to catch! I screamed a long time before I even got you to hear me."

"I'm in a hurry, Carlo. I shouldn't have stopped at all. But when you kept running and screaming like that, I figured Mac had sent you, so I stopped."

"Well, you can come with me now to the park," Carlo said.

"I told Mac last week I couldn't play. I gotta watch the store while my dad makes deliveries."

"Oh, Mac understands," Carlo said. "Mac understands all that. But he told you today was the big game. You said you'd make some arrangements."

"I said I'd try. Well, I tried, and I couldn't. Listen, Carlo, I can't stand here arguing with you. I want to play in that game more than you want me to play in it. But I can't. I just can't." I turned and began walking up the street. "My dad's going to string me up as it is, I'm already so late."

Carlo followed. Like a terrier, once he got hold of something, he didn't let go. "I don't see what's so bad, just for one day," he insisted. "Just for one day Sheldon or Evelyn could cover for you."

"That's what I said, dummy," I insisted. "Don't you think I had the brains to say all that? But Pop said it wouldn't be just one day. He said there'd be a big game next week and another one the week after. And you know he's right about that. Then he said baseball isn't important."

"He's wrong about that," Carlo said.

"That's what you and I think," I pointed out. "That's not what he thinks."

Carlo tried one last time. "We need you, Benny. Boy, do we need you."

"No, you don't," I said. "You got Mac, you don't need no one else."

"Mac says we need you."

"Do you think you need me?" I asked.

Carlo shrugged. "Yeah," he replied. "I guess so."

"Lookit, Carlo," I said, "just stop it now. I gotta go." And I began to run. This time Carlo didn't follow me.

As soon as I entered the store, my father came out from behind the counter. He already had his coat on. "Benny, Benny," he said. "The ladies that give me orders over the phone want the food in time to make dinner. If you don't get here until quarter to four, how am I going to make the deliveries in time?" It was the same old story.

I hung my jacket on the coat rack at the back of the store and put on my white apron. "I'm sorry, Pop. Carlo stopped me. I ran all the way."

My father nodded. "I can see that," he said. I could feel the locks of hair that had fallen down over my sweaty forehead. Beads of sweat had formed on my upper lip too. The morning had been cool, but it had turned into another warm day.

"Go wash your face and comb your hair," Pop ordered. "Another two minutes isn't going to make any difference." Inside the little bathroom at the back of the store, I could still hear him talking. "Why should a woman shop in a little grocery store like mine instead of the A&P, where the prices are lower? Only because I give her the kind of service the A&P can't give her. She calls me up, I deliver." When I came out of the bathroom, washed and combed, he was still talking. "But Benny, if you're not here, I can't deliver."

"I'm sorry Pop," I said again. "I told you. Carlo stopped me."

"Next time, don't stop for Carlo." He walked out of the store. I stood by the window and watched him drive away. Then I sat down on the stepladder behind the counter and pulled out a Hebrew book. Of course, much as I hated working in the store, I liked it better than Hebrew school. If it weren't for my bar mitzvah, I'd have quit altogether, no matter what my father and mother said. But I wanted to be bar mitzvah. They got you long pants for your bar mitzvah. Boys who weren't Jewish had to wait until they graduated from eighth grade to get long pants.

I opened the Hebrew book and began to read the words out loud. I didn't know what they meant. Trying to read words that have no meaning is the most boring thing of all. Luckily, I was interrupted twice by customers. First Billy McGee from the apartment house across the street came in to buy a loaf of bread and a quart of milk for his mother. He told me to charge it. I knew Pop didn't like to charge for the McGees, who hadn't paid their bill in three months, but Billy was seventeen and twice my size, so I didn't feel like arguing with him. The second customer was a woman I'd never seen before. She bought a jar of Ovaltine, a can of Campbell's vegetable soup, a small box of saltine crackers, a pound of margarine with a little packet of dye to turn it yellow, and a two-cent pickle out of the barrel. She paid cash.

No other customers came. It was a slow afternoon, and very warm too. I found it harder and harder to concentrate on Hebrew. I had another book, which Sheldon had given me. He had gotten it for his bar mitzvah. He had said it would be a good thing if I knew something about the religion I was getting into. The book was called *The Wisdom of the Sages*. I had never even opened it before, but for lack of anything better to do, I thumbed through it. Something hit my eye, something Rabbi Hillel said a thousand or so years ago. Who would think such an old guy would have been so smart? He said, "If I am not for myself, who will be for me? If I am for myself alone, of what use am I?" I read some more of the book to see if there were any other smart sayings like that, but there weren't. I mean, there were, but they didn't get to me that particular day.

Finally I put the book away, got up, and took an apple out of the barrel. It was mealy, but I ate it anyway. Then I took the feather duster off the coat rack and began to dust the cans on the shelves, even though I'd done that yesterday. I liked to get up on the stepladder to dust the ones at the top.

I was on the highest rung of the ladder when I heard the little bell that rang every time the door opened. "Just wait a sec," I called. "Be right there."

"Oh, take it easy," a boy's voice replied, heavy with sarcasm. "I got all the time in the world."

thirteen

It was Mac. I scrambled down off the ladder as fast as I could. "Mac, what're you doing here? Why aren't you at that game?"

"I postponed the game," Mac said. "The game ain't beginning until four forty-five. If we run, we can make it."

"You know I can't leave the store," I said. I felt like crying.

"I came to talk to your dad about that," Mac said. "If I talk to him, maybe he'll change his mind."

If Mac talked to him, maybe he would. Mac was the most persuasive person I'd ever met. But it was too late for that now. "Pop isn't here," I said. "He's out making deliveries."

"Call upstairs. Get one of them to come down."

That was the worst idea Mac had ever had. But I couldn't explain all that to him. I just said no. "I can't. Watching the store is *my* job."

Mac looked around. When we stopped talking, the place was silent as a tomb. There weren't even any people passing on the hot, still street. "What's there to watch?" he asked. "There ain't no one here. You got a key?"

"There's one in the cash register." The words tumbled out of my mouth before I even realized it. Pop had told me never to mention to anyone where the extra set of keys was kept.

"Then lock the place up and come with me," Mac said.

"Mac, I can't do that," I insisted. "You know I can't do that."

"I'll tell you what I do know," Mac said slowly in a low, hard voice. "I know you promised me last week that you'd play in this game. Just this one game. It's all I care about. And you promised."

"Mac," I began to explain, "I didn't promise. I said I'd try. Well, I did try. And I can't."

"You break a promise to me," Mac said, "and I don't ever speak to you again. If you're *lucky*, I don't ever speak to you again." He didn't raise his voice. He didn't have to.

I turned away and picked up the feather duster,

aimlessly dragging it along the top of the counter. "You know, Benny," he went on, "the worst thing is a welsher. A welsher is the very worst thing of all. You promised, and now you turn out to be a welsher."

"I'm no welsher, Mac. I promised my father too."

Mac shrugged. "It's up to you, Benny. I gotta go now. If we don't start that game in five minutes, we forfeit. Not that it'll matter much. If you're not there, we'll lose anyway."

I stood absolutely still, staring at him. Henry had said Mac needed me. Carlo had said Mac needed me. I hadn't really trusted them. But if Mac himself said it—well, that was different.

"You really believe that?" I asked, clenching the feather duster tight in my fist.

"Sure I believe it," Mac said calmly. "It's true."

I put down the feather duster and untied my apron. I folded it neatly and tucked it under the counter. I didn't bother with my jacket. It was too warm for it anyway. "I can't go upstairs to get my glove," I said. "My mother and sister will want to know why I'm not in the store."

"You can use Carlo's glove," Mac said. "He don't need it."

I punched *NO SALE* on the cash register and removed the key from the little covered compartment in the back. Mac and I walked out of the store together. I locked the door and dropped the key

110

in my pocket. We ran all the way to the park. We got there just in time. One of the boys from the YMCA had a wristwatch, so he knew.

Luckily the YMCA was right near the park, so the YMCA boys counted as the home team and the visitors were up first. That gave Mac and me a few minutes to rest. The YMCA boys were good. They had two seventh graders on their team, and this other big kid who said he was in sixth grade, but if he was, it must have been for the third time.

The YMCA pitcher struck out the guys from Albert Payson Terhune, one two three. Neither Mac nor I even came up to bat. Then the YMCA team got two runs in the bottom of the first inning. Mac was still tired from his ten-block run back to the park. When he came up to bat in the second inning, he struck out. I got a base hit and so did Carlo. But before we could score, we were back in the field. The next four innings were pretty much the same —this one on base and that one on base, but no scoring on either side. Mac had recovered his wind, and the YMCA was finding it harder and harder to get hits off him.

But the YMCA pitcher was good, too, and we weren't getting anywhere with him either. And for us, it mattered, because we didn't have any two runs in the kitty for insurance.

Finally, though, in the top of the eighth, the pitcher began to tire a little. I had been waiting

111

for that to happen. I hit the ball hard and true, sending it right through the trees beyond the baseball diamond, almost all the way to the lake. When I hit a ball like that, I had the same feeling of being unbeatable, of being powerful and free, that I had had the day I rode the bridge above the river.

I didn't even have to run. I trotted all the way around the bases, just like Babe Ruth in his prime, while the YMCA left fielder went careening down through the woods, looking for the ball.

There was a close call in the bottom of the eighth. Mac gave up one walk and two base hits, but he managed to get the YMCA team out before anyone could score. Then Double Dip and Carlo and Mac all got base hits in the top of the ninth. Fred and a kid named Mickey Michaelson had struck out by the time it was my turn at bat. Again I cracked the ball out toward left field. I ran like a bear was chasing me and made a two-bagger out of it. Mac and Carlo both scored. That was the game. The YMCA couldn't do a thing in the bottom of the ninth.

"Beefed up your team a little since the last time, didn't ya?" the YMCA pitcher said to Mac when the game was over. "No wonder you made us wait. We won't do that again."

"You gonna play us again, or are you too chicken?" Mac replied.

"We ain't chicken." The pitcher spit out the words. "Next Tuesday?"

"We got a game next Tuesday. And next Thursday too. But we'll see you the Tuesday after that if you want."

The pitcher nodded. "A week from Tuesday. You gonna need more than him," he said, pointing to me, "to beat us then."

Mac punched my shoulder. The pitcher ran after the rest of his team, who were making a lot of noise as they left the park. They didn't want us thinking they were upset or anything.

"Come on, Benny," Mac said. "I'll walk part of the way home with you. It's a darn good thing I made you come. Those punks woulda beat us again if I hadn't. I'll walk you all the way home. It's only a coupla blocks outta my way."

"No," I said, "don't do that. I gotta run." Before Mac could say another word, I took off. All the time I had been playing the game, I hadn't thought about anything except the game. Even when I'd heard the bell in the church tower strike six, I hadn't thought about anything but the game. Now, though, I began to think about other things. There had been a lot of cardboard cartons in the truck. Maybe Pop had had so many deliveries that he wasn't back yet. Maybe I could get home and open up the store again before he even knew that it had been closed.

But when I reached the corner of Main and Park, I saw the light on in the store. My father had gotten there first, of course. Really, I had known that was how it would be.

fourteen

I pushed open the door of the store slowly. Mr. Edelstein and Mr. Growtowski were both inside. Pop always kept the store open until six-thirty, or even a little later, to catch the coming-home-from-work trade.

When he heard the bell, Pop looked up from the cash register where he was ringing up Mr. Edelstein's order. "Go upstairs, Benjamin," he said.

"Can't I help you, Pop?" I asked, even though I was nervous as a cat. My father *never* called me *Benjamin*.

"I said go upstairs. Wait for me there."

I stepped back out into the street and closed the door behind me. I opened the door that led to the apartment. I climbed the stairs as slowly as if I were carrying three cases of Campbell's soup cans.

Sheldon was in the living room, studying at the desk. I could hear Evelyn out in the kitchen, getting dinner ready and talking to Ma, who, I knew, must be sitting in the big rocker in the corner.

I tiptoed very, very quietly through the living room. If I didn't make a sound, maybe I could get to the bedroom before anyone even knew I'd come in.

But Sheldon had some kind of sixth sense so far as I was concerned. "So, you finally decided to come home, did you?" he said, without even looking up.

I stopped in my tracks. Sheldon turned slowly around in his chair. "Geez, is Pop mad at you," he said. "Boy, are you going to get it."

"Benny, is that you?" Ma's voice called shrilly from the kitchen.

There was no escaping her now. Besides, compared with Sheldon, Ma was the lesser of two evils. I walked slowly through the living room and dining room into the kitchen.

"Benny," Ma said before I even got through the door, "how could you do a thing like that? How could you? You know how sick I am. Everyone else is trying to help. But you have to go and do a thing like that."

Evvie didn't say anything. She just stirred the

pot of stew on the stove with a big wooden spoon.

"I'm sorry, Ma," I said. "I didn't mean to. . ."

"What do you mean, you didn't mean to?" my mother interrupted angrily. "You certainly can't call leaving the store and locking the door behind you an accident! Your father is going to have to really do something to you for this. This time he's really going to have to do something."

"I'm hungry," I said. "Can I have something to eat?"

"Something to eat? Something to eat?" Ma was furious. "You want something to eat, at a time like this? After what you've done?"

"Ma, don't get yourself excited," Evvie said. "You know it isn't good for you."

"Not get excited? With a son like this, how can I not get excited? I can't figure out what God had in mind, giving me a son like this." She pulled her old brown cardigan sweater closer to her body and shook her head.

I heard my father come into the living room. "Benny's in the kitchen," Sheldon said in a loud, clear voice. "What are you going to do to him, Pop?"

"Don't you worry about Benny," Pop said. "I'll take care of him." Then he came into the kitchen. Sheldon followed.

"Well, Jake," Ma said as soon as she saw him, "you'll have to punish Benny this time. This time you'll certainly have to punish him."

"I'll take care of Benny," Pop repeated. He said it in almost exactly the same way he'd said it to Sheldon.

"You'll change your mind," Sheldon said. "He'll get around you, like he always does. But he's not a baby anymore. He should learn that he can't get away with everything forever."

"Sheldon, suppose you just get out of here for a little while. Go back to your books. You go too, Evvie."

"But, Pop," Evelyn protested, "I've got to finish setting the table."

"The table can wait a few minutes. No one's eating yet anyway. Go ahead, Evvie." Evvie and Sheldon walked out of the kitchen. The sound of their footsteps ceased in the dining room. "All the way," Pop called. "Into the sun parlor." Then he turned and stared at me in that sad way he had which always made me feel so terrible. For a minute he didn't say anything. Ma started in all over again about how I would send her to an early grave, but I hardly heard her.

"I have to punish you, Benny," Pop said at last. "You know that, don't you?"

"Yes," I replied.

He went right on. "You told me yesterday you were going to make me proud of you. Is this how you do it? By disobeying me? By deliberately disobeying my exact instructions? Just for a baseball game?"

117

"But it wasn't just an ordinary game," I pointed out. Not that I expected him to understand.

"Don't interrupt me, Benny. I think I heard everything you had to say on that subject yesterday. You obviously have no sense of what really matters in this world. While the rest of us go to the World's Fair on Sunday, you can stay home and study your arithmetic. Perhaps that will teach you."

I felt as if the bottom of my stomach had opened up and all my insides had fallen out, up to and including my heart. That was gone too. "But Pop," I cried, "can't you think of something else? That's not right. The fair was my idea."

"In this life, Benny," my father said, "everything has a price. The price of that ball game was the World's Fair. Now you can decide if it was worth the price."

"But Pop, that's not right," I repeated. "I didn't know in advance!"

"We never do, Benny. We never know what the price will be in advance. It's good to learn now that the price of a moment of pleasure is always very high."

I knew that the ball game wasn't a "moment of pleasure." But what it really was my father could never know. I turned to my mother. Her bark had always been a lot worse than her bite. "Ma, it isn't fair."

"Listen, Jake," Ma said, "maybe something else.

Maybe take away his movie money for the next month. For the next six months."

"Gertie, please. Leave this to me. Can't you see that missing his movies and ice cream for a few weeks won't mean a thing to him? It has to be something he really cares about if he's to learn anything from all of this."

"I think he's learned already. Haven't you, Benny?" she asked, turning to me.

I didn't say anything.

"I'm not so sure he has," Pop said.

"Pop. . ." I began.

He raised his hand. "That's all, Benny. I have nothing more to say." He pushed himself away from the kitchen table and stood up. "Go tell Evvie she can finish getting supper. I'm going to wash up."

He walked out of the kitchen and I turned once again to my mother. "Can't you do something? It's not right."

"I'll try," my mother said. "After he's had his dinner we'll talk to him. We'll tell him that you really have learned your lesson and that you'll never do anything like that again. You must make it very, very clear to him that you will never, ever disobey him, certainly not over a silly baseball game. If he really believes you, I think he'll forgive you. I really do. He just has to understand how sorry you are."

But I wasn't really sorry. I was sorry that I had disobeyed him, sorry that I had caused the terrible sad look in his eyes. But I wasn't sorry that I had played in that baseball game. Baseball was something I did, not just something I saw. Pop had said you pay a price for everything in this life. Well, it occurred to me at that moment that the feeling I had when my bat connected with a flying ball was worth a lot. It might possibly even be worth a trip to the World's Fair, though I wasn't sure.

"I'm not sorry I played in the game," I told my mother. "I won't say that I am, and I won't say that I'll never play in a game again."

Ma struck her hand to her forehead. "Oy vey," she sighed. "You are the stubbornest boy I ever met. You'll be the death of me yet. If you're not sorry, if you won't promise never to do it again, how can you expect him to let you go to the fair?"

"All right," I said. "I won't go."

Sheldon came strolling into the kitchen with Evvie behind him. "Well," he asked, "what did he say? He didn't hit you."

"Oh, Sheldon, don't be ridiculous," Evvie said. "He's never hit any of us. Why should he start now?"

"We never did anything this bad," Sheldon said.

"I wish he had hit me," I said. "I wish he had hit me with his belt. With the buckle end, like Henry's old man does sometimes."

"Well, what did he do?" Evvie asked. "What could be worse?"

I looked her in the eye. "I can't go to the fair Sunday. I have to stay home and do arithmetic."

Even Sheldon was silent for a moment when he heard that. Evvie was the first to speak. "Oh, Benny," she said softly, "that's too much."

"Yeah," I agreed. "That's what I said."

"But you do deserve it," Sheldon said in his most reasonable tone. "Even you have to admit that, Benny. Leaving the store was a terrible thing. And for what? For a baseball game! It would have been different if you were rescuing a kid from a fire or something. But a baseball game?"

"Oh, shut up, Sheldon!" I cried out suddenly. "You don't know anything about it." He made me so mad, madder than anyone else could.

"What do you mean?" Sheldon protested in that same infuriatingly reasonable tone. "I used to like baseball too. But I always knew it was just a game."

I stood up. "I don't think I want any supper," I said.

Ma looked at me. "When you first came in, you were so hungry. You better eat something."

"I'm not hungry anymore." I started for the kitchen door. As I passed Sheldon, I paused. "You know what you can do for me, Sheldon?" I asked in my pleasantest voice.

"What?" Sheldon rose to the bait.

"You can go to hell!" It sure was good to say that at last.

"Benny!" my mother cried. But I didn't stay to listen. I ran to our bedroom and shut the door. A few moments later I heard Sheldon rattling the knob, but he couldn't get in. I had locked it, from the inside.

fifteen

"Don't come downstairs to say good-bye to us,"
Pop said to me on Sunday. He held his good gray
hat in one hand and the keys to the truck in the
other. Ma was in the living room too, wearing her
navy blue silk spring coat, and a navy blue straw
hat with cherries on the brim. She hadn't been so
dressed up since Rosh Hashanah, the Jewish New
Year, the previous September. Right after that she'd
gotten sick.

Sheldon was already down in the truck, blowing
the horn. Evvie and Morty Katz had left earlier.

123

They were taking a train into Manhattan and then a subway out to Flushing Meadows. They were going to meet the rest of the family by the big cash register at eleven o'clock.

I was sitting at the desk in the living room, the one Sheldon usually sat at. I had my arithmetic book open in front of me and my Hebrew books piled behind it. I didn't want to turn around to look at them. "Don't worry," I said, making no effort to keep the bitterness I felt out of my voice. "If I come down to say good-bye, I won't run away after you're gone. You can trust me."

"That's not what Pop means," my mother tried to explain. "He doesn't want you to feel worse than you already do. If you watch us go, you'll feel worse." She came over to the desk and kissed me on top of the head. I didn't turn around or look up. "There's plenty of fruit in the ice-box," she said. "You can make yourself a salami sandwich for lunch. For supper you can have the leftover chicken from Friday night."

"O.K., Ma," I muttered.

"Don't be so mad at us, Benny," Ma said in a low voice. "It's really your fault, you know, that you're not going."

"I never said it wasn't."

"Come on, Gertie," my father said. "Let's get going. Good-bye, Benny."

"Well, good-bye," Ma added.

"So long." Still I did not turn around or get up. Down below, Sheldon honked the horn of the truck once again. I heard them clatter out of the door and down the steps, and a few moments later, through the open windows of the sun parlor, came the sound of the truck pulling away from the curb.

Immediately I got up, went to the icebox, and picked some grapes off the bunch in a bowl on one of the shelves. I did not cut a little branch off with a scissors the way I was supposed to. By the time the day was over, there'd probably be just a bare skeleton left in the bowl. I didn't care.

I ambled back into the living room. I didn't sit down at the desk. My father would expect to see some pieces of arithmetic paper covered with attempts to solve problems when he came back from the fair, but there was plenty of time for that. Hours and hours. I had been expressly forbidden to leave the house, and I knew I would not disobey. Ma might call sometime during the day. She wasn't crazy about the idea of leaving me all alone even if I was twelve and a half.

I picked up the *Sunday News* from the end table and began to read the comics. It was odd to be holding the entire comic section in my own hands, and not to be fighting with Evvie and Sheldon for little pieces of it. Sheldon always insisted on reading the comics in order. Evvie was willing to take the section apart, read one whole four-sided page at a time, and then pass it on. Not Sheldon. If he got to the comics first, he read them all before he'd give another person any. Today I could do that. It didn't turn out to be so great. I used to think it'd be heaven to be an only child. Here I was, less than an hour into it, and I was bored to death. Of course, it would have been different if I could have gone out, but I couldn't. Or if my parents were home, but they weren't.

I put down the paper and walked to the open windows in the sun parlor. Down below, people were doing Sunday morning things. They were going into the bakery for buns, or into the candy store for the Sunday paper, or walking up the street, dressed in their leftover Easter clothes, to St. Anne's on the corner of Main and Chestnut. Everyone but me had somewhere to go.

I went back to the comics. I read "Dick Tracy," "Gasoline Alley," "Moon Mullins," "Terry and the Pirates," "Winnie Winkle," and all the others. I even read "Little Orphan Annie," which I hated because it had so many words and seemed incredibly stupid besides. I had just put down the comics and picked up the rotogravure when the telephone rang. Next to the doorbell, it was the most welcome sound I could have heard. I ran into the hall to answer it. It was Goldie.

"Benny," she said. "Let me talk to your father. Or your mother." She sounded terribly out of breath.

"They're not here, Goldie. Don't you remember? They went to the World's Fair today. I didn't go. I'm being punished."

Ordinarily, Goldie would have wanted to hear all about it. As a matter of fact, there had been times in the previous week when I had thought of calling her up and telling her. But today she didn't seem to pay any attention to me. "Oy vey," she said. "What am I going to do now?"

"What's the matter?" I was worried. I had never heard Goldie sound so upset.

She sighed heavily. "We can't find Arnulf. We think he's run away."

I was surprised to realize I was not surprised. "When?" I asked.

"He never came down for breakfast this morning," Goldie began. "Of course, that's not unusual. The girls knocked on his door. They didn't get any answer so finally I went up myself. He didn't answer me either, so I got mad, and pushed on the door. It wasn't even locked. He wasn't there. So we don't know when he left—sometime last night or early in the morning."

"You should have called me before," I said. "You should have told me right away."

"Why?" Goldie apparently was so amazed by what I'd said that for the moment her voice forgot to sound upset. "What can you do?"

I tried to explain. "Arnulf and me—we get along," I said.

"Get along!" Goldie exclaimed. "Arnulf doesn't get along with anyone."

"Well," I said, "we talked. We talked about quite a few things last Sunday."

"Like what?" Goldie asked. "Maybe you'll give me a clue."

"Like his family," I answered. "And then I sat on his bed and he told me about chemistry."

Suddenly, in my mind's eye, I could see *The New York Times* lying open on Arnulf's red and white chenille bedspread, folded over to the column headed *Shipping and Mails*. You know how in the comics when someone gets an idea they show a light bulb in the balloon where the words usually are? I felt just like that—just as if a light bulb had turned on in my head. "My God," I shouted excitedly, "I bet I know where he is!"

Goldie got just as excited as I was. "Where? Where?" she cried.

"There's probably a ship sailing for Germany today," I explained. "I bet he's down at the pier, trying to get on it somehow. He followed the shipping news. I know, because I saw the paper in his bedroom last Sunday. I wondered why then. Now I think I know. I bet you anything he's trying to get on some ship."

"That's crazy," Goldie said. "Why would he want to do a crazy thing like that?"

"Well, you know how homesick he was . . . is . . . was."

"No," said Goldie. "I didn't know."

"Cripes, Goldie," I exclaimed, "he made it perfectly clear. Didn't you ever listen to him?"

"Maybe I didn't," Goldie admitted softly. "He threw my house into such an uproar, I guess I was just too mad at him to listen to him. Anyway," she added, with a return to her usual confident tone of voice, "I just can't imagine any Jew being homesick for Hitler's country. If he is, he's even crazier than I thought."

"He's not homesick for Hitler, for heaven's sake." I was kind of annoyed at Goldie's sudden stupidity. "He's not even homesick for Germany. He's homesick for *home*. You knew he missed his family."

"Well, of course. But to try to go back. . ."

"Did you call the police?"

"Yes," Goldie replied. "We called them a little while ago. First Moe and the girls looked for him in the neighborhood and I phoned the people in Philadelphia, and everyone else he knew."

"Since he didn't like anyone he knew, it wasn't likely he'd go to any of their houses."

"Now that I think of it, he did mention you once or twice," Goldie commented thoughtfully. "He said when his experiment was all set up he was going to call you to come see it work. He said you'd promised to come over on the streetcar. I should have called you before."

"That's what I said," I reminded her. "I don't think," I added, "that it's such a good idea for the police to go after him down at the pier. We don't want him to think we think he's some kind of criminal."

"All right," Goldie said. "I'll call them and tell them we have a lead we're going to follow out ourselves, and they should keep looking."

"Yes," I agreed. I felt like William Powell in a Thin Man movie. I remembered what my father had said about not leaving the house all day, but I dismissed it. Finding Arnulf seemed to me to be like the rescue of a child from a fire that Sheldon had talked about. It was reason enough to go out. "Do you have today's *Times?*" I asked Goldie. "I don't think the *News* has sailing information."

"No," Goldie replied. "We never had a chance to go out and get it this morning."

"While you're driving over to pick me up, I'll run out and get a copy. That way we can find out if there are any ships sailing for Germany today. Of course, they'd be in yesterday's paper, if you have that."

"No," Goldie said, "usually we only get the *Times* on Sunday. Not too many ships sail on Sunday."

"But it's possible," I said.

"It's possible," Goldie agreed. "Maybe they want to squeeze in one last trip before the new taxes on German imports take effect. Go ahead. Go get a paper while we come for you. We'll look around the piers, even if there are no sailings. Who knows what craziness that boy's thinking of?"

130

When she hung up, I realized she sounded a hundred percent better than she had when she first called. If Goldie was in trouble, she wanted to be doing something about it, even if what she was doing turned out to be nothing more than a wild-goose chase.

But I didn't believe that it would turn out to be a wild-goose chase. I was convinced that Arnulf was at some pier, trying somehow to board a ship for Germany. As I ran down to the candy store, I thought again that I was disobeying my father. Well, whatever the punishment, I'd have to bear it. I wasn't going to let Goldie and Moe go for Arnulf without me. I could talk to Arnulf only a little, but they couldn't talk to him at all.

sixteen

We didn't say much to each other during the ride into New York City. I was glad the girls had had the sense to stay home. I took the paper with me and while we were driving, I read Moe and Goldie the shipping news. "SAILS TODAY. *Transatlantic. Goldheim* (Hanseatic) Hamburg, May 27. Pier 59, Eighteenth St., 11:00 A.M." That was the only one.

"We'll never make it," Goldie said. "It's after eleven already."

"I don't think we have to worry about that," Moe assured her. "There's no way Arnulf can get on that ship. You read stories about stowaways, but to do it in real life is almost impossible."

"Arnulf is pretty smart," I said. "He might be able to figure out a way."

Moe parked the car on Eleventh Avenue and we walked as quickly as we could up the wooden walk, through the wide doors, and into a huge, cavernous room. It was nearly empty. Here and there, two or three people sat on benches, talking. A porter was pushing a cart loaded with wooden crates. Another one was sweeping the floor.

Moe and Goldie went to find a policeman or an official of the steamship line or someone else who could help us in some way. But I walked up and down the rows of benches, which were high-backed, like pews in a church. And on one of them, scrunched up in a corner so that I could not see him from behind, was Arnulf. Next to him on the bench was a large shopping bag from Bamberger's department store, full to bursting. As for Arnulf, he was asleep. His face was dirty, and the dirt was streaked, as if he had been crying.

I sat down on the bench, the Bamberger's bag between us. "Wake up, Arnulf," I said softly. "Wake up."

Arnulf stirred, but his eyes remained shut. I reached out and touched his shoulder, shaking him gently. "Wake up, Arnulf, wake up. We can go home now."

Arnulf opened his eyes slowly. He blinked for a moment or two, and then he said, "Hello, Benny."

"Hello, Arnulf. How are you?" I replied as calmly as I could.

"I'm all right," Arnulf said.

I took my handkerchief out of my pocket. Ma insisted that I always carry one. "Here, blow your nose. You're all snotty."

"Thanks." Arnulf took the handkerchief and wiped his face. Actually, he only smudged the dirt worse.

"You couldn't get on, huh?" I asked.

"I didn't even try," he replied. "If I had, they'd have caught me and turned me over to the police, and Mr. and Mrs. Glaser would have found me before this. But once I got here, I didn't even try."

"You meant to, though. You brought your stuff." I touched the shopping bag. "You know, Arn, you shouldn't have done it. You worried them so much. Don't you think, if you want to go back so bad, it could be set up? If you told your folks you didn't care about the danger, you just wanted to be with them, they'd let you come home. I bet they would."

Suddenly Arnulf's eyes filled up with tears. "What's the matter?" I asked. I was upset. Here I was, trying to comfort him, and instead, he was crying again.

"Benny, you don't understand," he sobbed. "I've written them that. I've written them that a thousand times. I haven't had a letter from them in more than a month." He began to cry uncontrollably and

134

could not go on. For a moment or two, he held his head in his hands, and didn't try to push back the tears. I put the shopping bag on the floor and moved next to him, lightly resting my hand on his shoulder.

After a while, he stopped crying. He blew his nose with my dirty handkerchief, and started talking again. "You see, I hadn't heard from them in so long, I told myself something must be wrong. Something must have happened to them, or they would have written. That's why I had this stupid idea of getting on this ship somehow. But when I got here, I couldn't fool myself anymore. They haven't written because they don't want me. It's not me they're afraid for. It's themselves. My father's afraid for his job. And my stepmother—she's just afraid. They don't want a Jew for a son. They don't even want a Jew for a correspondent, four thousand miles away."

I had never heard of anything so terrible. I had never heard of a father who really and truly didn't want his own son. I didn't know what to say. I pulled a piece of chewing gum out of my pocket. Its package had long ago disappeared and it was kind of bent double and squished, but it was all I had. I held it out to Arnulf without saying anything. He took it and picked at the wrapper, which was stuck to the gum, just as carefully as he had fooled around with his wires, tubing, and glass bottles.

Goldie, Moe, and a man I didn't know came out

of a door in the far corner of that huge barn of a room. I was glad to see them because I couldn't think of a single thing to say to Arnulf after what he'd said to me. I couldn't comfort him, because what he said sounded like the truth, and how could you comfort a person for that?

I stood up on the bench and waved. "Here," I called. "We're over here." I had to shout several times before they noticed me, but then they hurried over.

The strange man wore a blue uniform with gold letters above the breast pocket which read *Hanseatic Lines*. He looked sternly at Arnulf. "If I were your father, young man," he said, "I'd take you home and give you the hiding of your life."

"You are not my father," Arnulf said, as prickly as ever in spite of the fact that his face was stained with tears. "I have no father."

"Of course you do," Moe said. "What are you talking about?"

But Goldie had seen his face. It was as if she had looked at it for the first time. "Thanks a lot," she said to the man from the steamship line. "Thanks for all your help. Now we have to go. We have to get this young man home." She put her hand under Arnulf's elbow and hoisted him out of his seat. "Let's go." Arnulf accompanied her without protest. Moe and I followed.

"Wait," called the man. "You have to come back

into the office. I must file a report. You have to fill out the forms."

Moe turned back to him. "Why?" he asked. "Nothing's happened. You didn't find the boy. Benny did. What's there to report?"

"But there are procedures. . . I must insist. . ."

"Call us up on the telephone," Moe said. He hurried after Goldie and Arnulf.

"I don't know your number," the man called after us desperately. "I don't even know your name." But we didn't stop again, or turn around, and after a moment, he gave up.

Once in the car, however, Moe could no longer hold back his anger. "Do you know what you did to us?" he asked Arnulf. "Do you have any idea?"

"You don't really care about what happens to me," Arnulf said. He didn't sound mad. He said it as if he were simply stating a fact. "Nobody does. Not one person in the whole wide world."

"Why, Arnulf," Goldie protested, "what a terrible thing to say. It isn't true. You know it isn't."

"Well," I pointed out, "I don't know if it's true or not, but if it seems true to him, then it might just as well be true. Isn't that so?"

"But we do care," Goldie insisted. "I wish there was some way we could show you that, Arnulf."

"They came after you," I told Arnulf. "They came after you themselves. They could have just sent the police." Arnulf didn't say anything. "Tell us how you did it," I continued. "How you planned it and everything."

"Nothing happened," Arnulf said. "It didn't work out."

"It could have, though," I said. "It was an adventure."

So Arnulf told his story, and as he did so, he got excited, and some of the sadness went out of him. His eyes grew bright and he gestured frequently as he spoke. I could tell he had enjoyed occupying his mind with his plans, even if they hadn't worked out.

"I didn't use all of the money Mr. Glaser gave me for my chemistry experiment," Arnulf said. "I saved some of it, and I had a little of the money left Papa gave me when I came. I've been reading the shipping news almost since I got to this country. I began just because I liked to read the names of the German vessels and the cities, like Bremen and Hamburg."

"There are plenty of German names in the rest of the newspaper too," Moe said with some bitterness.

"I do not enjoy reading about Chancellor Hitler," Arnulf replied formally. "You misunderstand me if you think I or my parents approve of Herr Hitler."

"Germany and Hitler—" Moe began.

"Are not the same thing," Arnulf interrupted.

"No?" Moe replied. "Then why—"

138

But Goldie would not let him continue. She put her hand on Moe's knee and said loudly, "You got the idea, maybe, of stowing away, from reading the shipping news?"

Arnulf nodded. "That is correct. So then I really began to read it carefully. I wanted to leave on a Sunday because everybody in America sleeps late Sunday and I could get a good head start. But very few ships sail on Sundays and it took me a while before I could find one. When I did, I put some things in a shopping bag." He shoved the Bamberger's bag on the floor with his foot. "I didn't want to carry too much, and I didn't want you to think I was gone for good. If all my clothes and suitcases were gone, you might think of the ship a lot sooner." He stopped for a moment. "I'm surprised how fast you did think of it," he added. His voice suggested that he had never been overwhelmed with their intelligence.

"It never would have occurred to us," Goldie admitted. "Benny thought of it."

Arnulf looked at me and nodded. "Ah, yes, Benny. Well, Benny is different." He didn't explain, but went on with his story. "And another thing—I never answered when you called me. I pretended I didn't hear."

"Or didn't want to hear," Moe mumbled, but no one heard him. At least we pretended we didn't hear him.

"That way," Arnulf pointed out, "you'd be used to my not answering when you called me, and it would be a while before you came to look for me, which would give me even more of a head start."

"But how did you know how to get into New York?" Goldie asked.

"That was easy. I took the train. One day when no one else was home I called up the station to find out the schedule. When I got to Pennsylvania Station in New York, I walked. New York is easy. All the streets are numbered in order. Not like a city in Europe. This morning I just got up as soon as it was light out and walked out of the house. I walked downtown and got on the first train, the 7:07."

"Who would think there'd be such an early train on a Sunday?" Goldie said.

"There was just one thing I didn't plan," Arnulf said. "The most important part."

"What's that?" Goldie asked.

"Actually getting on the ship," Arnulf replied, quiet now, the liveliness gone from his face. "I had sort of imagined myself trailing up the gangplank, behind some big family, where I wouldn't be noticed. But when I got to the pier, I couldn't do that. There were no big families. It was just a freighter, with only a few passengers. So I sat down on a bench and cried like a three-year-old. Why couldn't I find a way on that boat? After I got there,

I didn't even try to think of a plan." Arnulf shook his head in self-disgust.

"Because you didn't want to anymore," I said. "You had thought of . . . of what you told me before—about your parents."

"What's that?" Goldie asked again.

Arnulf didn't answer and I shot her a warning glance. "Maybe Arnulf will tell you about it someday," I said. "If he ever wants to, maybe he'll tell you."

"I really didn't expect you to get to me so quickly," Arnulf said. "I thought it was very possible you would not come after me at all."

"My God!" Goldie exclaimed. "Of course we came after you. We're responsible for you. Don't you understand that?" Then she added softly, "We're glad to have you back, Arnulf. Believe me, we are."

Arnulf shook his head. "You don't have to say that."

"It's true," Goldie insisted. "Someday you'll know." She moved her hand toward him. If she had been sitting in the back seat next to him, she would have hugged him, and that would have been a good thing, except maybe Arnulf wasn't ready for that yet.

"You have Essie and Sylvia," Arnulf said. "You have such a happy family. You don't need another person. . ." His voice trailed off.

I knew the rest of the sentence, the part he couldn't say out loud, ". . . a person whose own parents don't even want him." Instead, he said, "I don't need anyone. I can look out for myself."

"Sure you can," Goldie said soothingly, before Moe could open his mouth. "But if you don't come back and stay in that room, I'll have to get another boarder, won't I, some stranger. Maybe he'll be dirty or loud. Better you. So we'll try. You'll try. We'll all try."

Arnulf sighed and leaned back. He was really tired. "All right," he said. Then he shut his eyes. We had to wake him up when we got back to Newark.

Arnulf had to tell the whole story over again to Essie and Sylvia. They said very little, just offering occasional clucks of amazement, almost admiration, at such a remarkable feat.

Then we all ate a lot of dinner, and then Arnulf fell asleep again on the sofa in the living room. Goldie didn't want to leave him, so Moe and Essie drove me home.

seventeen

It was after eight when my mother and father and Sheldon and Evvie and Morty Katz came clattering up the stairs. They had all come home together, Morty and Sheldon agreeing to ride in the back of the truck, and, boy, were they surprised to find Moe and Essie in our apartment. They were also surprised to see me in such good shape. Well, of course I would have been kind of gloomy if I'd really stayed in the house all day.

Everyone talked at once, and it was a long time before they heard the whole story of my day and I

143

heard the whole story of theirs. "In the Perisphere they flash moving pictures on the ceiling," Sheldon said. "The ceiling's curved too. Can you imagine standing inside a ball?"

"We went to Billy Rose's Aquacade," Ma said. "I never saw a show like that. Those swimmers, they're like dancers."

"The line was too long at General Motors," Pop said. "We didn't want to spend our whole day waiting in line, so we saved that one for next time."

"Listen," Evvie said, "I saw so many unforgettable things, I can't begin to remember them." She paused for a moment, and smiled at me. "But it would have been better," she said, "if you'd been there."

"It's just a good thing he wasn't," Moe said. "We would never have thought of checking the steamship lines for Arnulf ourselves. It took us a long time to even think of calling the people in Philadelphia. We were too stunned to think at all, if you want to know the truth."

"Benny is a regular hero," Sheldon said, lifting his eyebrows.

Moe didn't catch the sarcasm. "Yes," he said, "that's just what he is. He understands a lot of things. He's a regular hero."

Later, after Moe and Essie had left, we had something to eat. Ma had invited Moe and Essie to join us, but they were anxious to get home. Morty Katz had to leave too, so only our family sat down at the table to eat the cherry cake Evvie had baked the day before. She made me tell them all over again what I had done that day. Even Sheldon listened.

Pop said, "You did all right. You acted like a *mensch*."

"Oh, well," Sheldon added, "no one ever doubted that Benny had a good heart. Do you know what a *mensch* is, Benny?"

"'If I am not for myself, who will be for me?'" I quoted. Sheldon looked surprised. "'If I am for myself alone, of what use am I?' That's in the book you gave me, Sheldon. That's a *mensch*. A human being."

"Do you want some coffee in your milk?" Ma asked. She'd never asked me that before. "Just to flavor it?"

"O.K.," I said. I wasn't sure I'd like it, but I was sure I'd drink it. Only grown-ups got to drink coffee in our house. Ma would give you wine long before she'd give you coffee.

"I had an idea," Pop said as he spooned sugar into his cup. "Maybe you could go to the fair next Sunday. You could go by train and subway. Morty and Evvie didn't have any trouble. Maybe a friend of yours would like to go too. Maybe Henry, or that Mac you're always talking about. You could even ask Arnulf. That is, if you wanted to."

"That sounds good, Pop," I replied. "I'd like to go to the fair, if not next Sunday, well, then, sometime. But there's something I'd like more."

"Oh? What's that?" Pop looked at me suspiciously.

"I want to play ball Tuesday afternoon after school," I said firmly. "With Mac and the other guys. It's an important game. Against some guys from the Southside."

"Oh, no," Sheldon muttered. "Not that all over again."

I was just about to stuff a piece of cherry cake into my mouth, but I didn't. Instead I turned toward Sheldon and shook it in his face. "You know what?" I said. "Baseball is important. It's very important. Studying is what you're good at, so that's what's important to you. But baseball is what I'm good at, so that's what's important to me!" Then I put the piece of cherry cake in my mouth and began to chew it, hard.

"Tuesday," Evelyn said, "I could watch the store. So what if the house weren't dusted just one day? I like to watch the store a lot better than cleaning the house anyway. And then, after the game, Benny could help me get a quick supper, like canned soup or something. And then he could help me wash up afterward."

"That's a very good idea," I said, my mouth still stuffed with cake. I had stopped chewing entirely while I listened to Evvie's marvelous suggestion. "I think that's the best idea I ever heard."

"Well, if you're going to take the afternoon off," Sheldon said, "you could put it to better use than playing ball. It would be a good time for me to help you with your arithmetic. You don't want to be left back, do you?"

What had made him say that, now, just when everything was beginning to go good? How did he know? "Who says I'm going to be left back?" I asked angrily.

"Mrs. Elfand. I met her in Doc Woronoff's Thursday. She told me to help with your arithmetic."

"Mrs. Elfand says Benny's going to be left back?" my mother moaned. "Oy, vey. Another thing to worry about."

"Well, she said *maybe* he's going to be left back," Sheldon admitted. "She didn't say for sure. She said I should help him, though. She definitely said that."

My heart sank. In spite of everything, I was going to lose again. I knew it.

"Sheldon," Pop asked mildly, "when was it you said you met Mrs. Elfand in the drugstore?"

"Thursday," Sheldon replied. I think it was Thursday. Maybe it was Wednesday. Wednesday or Thursday. I was there for Ma both days."

"Wednesday or Thursday, and today's Sunday. How come you waited until now to mention it?"

Sheldon shrugged. "Well, I don't know. . . ." He hesitated. "Benny seemed to be in enough trouble as it was. Besides, I really don't have much time for tutoring him, you know."

"The only time you have," I said, "is the very same time I want to play in that baseball game." I could have murdered him as easy as talk to him. Easier.

"It's not I who have that time," Sheldon told me. "It's *you!*"

"Sheldon, you're right," Pop said. "Arithmetic is more important than baseball. But I agree with Benny too. Your timing is a little odd. Because of Evvie's kind offer, Benny, this week you can play in your ball game Tuesday. Sheldon, you'll work with him on his arithmetic after supper."

"But Pop," Sheldon protested, "I can't spare the time. That's when I go to the library."

"Then how come you can spare Tuesday afternoon? Go to the library then. It's open." Sheldon had no reply to that. "You can find half an hour twice a week after supper to help Benny," Pop continued. "I know you can, a smart boy like you."

"All right," Sheldon agreed grudgingly. "I don't want him to fail. How would it look if my brother failed? But I can't give him any more than half an hour. That's all I've got."

"Half an hour will be ample," Pop assured him. "If at the end of that half hour neither you nor Benny is dead, we'll all of us consider ourselves very lucky!"

eighteen

Tuesday after school I went to the park with Mac's gang to play some kids from the Southside. Very tough guys, Mac said. It would be more important to play the following week, when there'd be a rematch with the guys from the YMCA, but I figured I'd better take the day I had, and worry about next week when next week came.

Once the game began, however, it became clear that Mac had been right to worry. Mac's gang had never played these guys before, and they were tough. Big and tough. They had four guys on their team as big as me.

By the seventh inning, we were down by two runs. The Southside boys' pitcher, a tall, skinny redhead, was really terrific. I wasn't able to get a single hit off him. The first time at bat, I hit a fly ball into left field. The second time, the catcher called out to the red-headed pitcher, "You don't got nothing to worry about. This kid's just a dumb ass." I knew that was only talk. Just regular heckling. That kid had never seen me before in his life. But I got all hot anyway, and struck out. It was humiliating. The other guys were disappointed. At the time, Fred was on third base, so they had expected something of me, and all they got was the third out.

As a matter of fact, we had crossed the plate only once in six whole innings. The score was three to one. If Mac himself had not been such a good pitcher, things would have been a lot worse. Mac had scored the single run, too, on hits by Carlo and Double Dip.

When I came up again in the bottom of the seventh, the situation was something like it had been my second time at bat. A little better—there was only one out instead of two. And a little worse —Fred was only on second base, not third.

The catcher was at it again. He had a mouth on him like an open sewer. "Here he comes, folks. Gargantua. The only ball-playing ape in the United States."

I turned around. I had a sudden, overwhelming

urge to knock the catcher over the head with my bat. "You got something to say, ape?" the catcher snarled at me.

But I had nothing to say. Because over the small hill behind the catcher, I could see a man walking slowly. A plump man, no more than five feet, six inches tall, with rounded shoulders and very little hair on top of his head. It was my father.

I could feel my mouth drop open. I didn't know what to think. Could it be that something had happened to Evelyn, or that he had changed his mind and was coming to take me back to the store? But no. When he saw me, he just smiled and waved. He yelled out something I couldn't catch.

"What?" I called back. "What did you say?"

By this time he was closer. "I'll watch a little," he shouted. "Go on with your game." He walked over and joined the small group standing behind the bench on which our team was sitting. Henry was there, and three or four girls from Mrs. Elfand's sixth grade, plus Double Dip's grandfather, who came to the park every dry afternoon, spring, summer, and fall. Two or three of his park bench friends were with him, rooting for the guys from the Southside, just to annoy him. I watched Pop shake hands with Double Dip's grandfather and stand next to him.

"You ready yet, ape?" the catcher asked. "We ain't got all day."

"Yeah, weasel," I said. "I'm ready." I took my

151

stance, feet apart, and lifted the bat to my shoulder.

The pitcher threw the ball. It was high, very high, but the umpire called, "Strike one." The umpire was a high school freshman the Southsiders had dug up somewhere.

"Whaddya mean, strike one?" Mac screamed, jumping up from the bench. "That ball woulda been high if Benny was ten feet tall."

"It was a strike," the catcher said. "D'ya wanna make something of it?"

"Let it go, Mac," I said. "Let it go this time."

"I'm not used to playing ball with cheats," Mac grumbled, but he sat down.

The catcher threw the ball back to the pitcher and again the pitcher threw the ball to me. This time it was good and I swung at it. I felt the bat connect, and I heard it too. I dropped it and started running. The ball sailed out to the left, over the outfielder's head, and I was safe on second base by the time he retrieved it and threw it in. Fred was safe too, at home plate.

The guys on the bench were screaming and so were the handful of fans. My father smiled and made a bull's-eye at me with his thumb and forefinger.

Mac and Abie Zaretski both hit singles, so I came in and tied the score before the inning was over. Then in the eighth Willy hit a home run. No one was on base, but it turned out not to matter. Mac didn't let a single Southsider on base in the top of the ninth and it was all over.

I rode home in the truck with Pop and Henry Silverberg. "I got done with my deliveries early," Pop explained, "so I thought I'd just drop by and see what was going on. It was a very good game. You boys play well. You take it very seriously."

"I think," Henry said, "that you have to take it seriously if you're going to play well."

My father nodded. "It's like anything else."

"Listen, Pop," I said, "thanks for coming. It was nice of you to take the time."

"I enjoyed it," he replied. "It was interesting."

"I think I'll call Arnulf up and ask him to come over and watch a game, sometime. If I play in any others."

"I guess you'll play in some others," Pop said. "If Evvie's willing, I guess we can spare you now and then."

"Arnulf can watch me play and I can listen to him explain chemistry experiments," I laughed. "Maybe I'll even get smart."

"The change in your attitude toward Arnulf is really remarkable," my father said. "I never realized that just when the rest of us really started to hate him, that's when you started to like him."

"I admire him," I explained.

"Admire him?" Henry asked.

"Yeah," I said. "He's tough. He fights back."

Illegitimus non carborundum. Don't let the bastards grind you down. No matter what went on in this world, things could never be as bad for me as they were for Arnulf. Not so long as I lived in the same house as my parents. Imagine Pop coming to a ball game. And Evvie minding the store for me so I could play. Even a brother like Sheldon was better than what Arnulf had. And Arnulf hadn't given in. Why should I?

About the Author

Barbara Cohen is also the author of *The Carp in the Bathtub; Thank You, Jackie Robinson; Where's Florrie?; and Bitter Herbs and Honey.* A teacher and a newspaper columnist, she lives in a small town in New Jersey with her husband Eugene and their three daughters, Leah, Sara, and Rebecca.